"I need help, Mommy. I can't twirl by myself."

Bailey started to rise from her chair.

"No," Mark said. "I'll help her twirl. You need to stay safely in that chair."

Bailey sat back down. She had to admit she wasn't used to having someone worry about her.

Soon the music was absorbing all Bailey's attention. Rosie was dancing her heart out, a big smile on her face and her copper-red curls bouncing in time with the song she had chosen. Mark seemed to instinctively know when a twirl was needed, and he held his hand out so he could steady Rosie in her moment of glory.

Bailey sighed as she saw her old friend gallantly help her daughter twist and turn. No matter what happened next in any of their lives, Bailey knew she would never forget this dance practice. Neither Mark nor her daughter was dressed in their finery, but the expressions of pure joy on each of their faces were perfect. They gave her hope for the future. Maybe having Mark for a friend would be enough for the both of them…

Janet Tronstad grew up on her family's farm in Montana and now lives in central California, where she is currently working on her next book. She has written over thirty books for Love Inspired, many of them set in the fictitious town of Dry Creek, Montana. When not writing, Janet loves to read, have lunch with friends and travel.

Books by Janet Tronstad

Love Inspired

Dry Creek

Visit the Author Profile page at Harlequin.com for more titles.

His Dry Creek Inheritance

Janet Tronstad

LOVE INSPIRED

INSPIRATIONAL ROMANCE

LOVE INSPIRED®
INSPIRATIONAL ROMANCE

PLEASE RECYCLE • THIS PRODUCT IS RECYCLABLE

Recycling programs for this product may not exist in your area.

ISBN-13: 978-1-335-55416-1

His Dry Creek Inheritance

Copyright © 2021 by Janet Tronstad

This edition published by arrangement with Harlequin Books S.A.

For questions and comments about the quality of this book, please contact us at CustomerService@Harlequin.com.

Love Inspired
22 Adelaide St. West, 40th Floor
Toronto, Ontario M5H 4E3, Canada
www.Harlequin.com

Printed in U.S.A.

And we know that all things work together for good to them that love God, to them who are the called according to his purpose.
—*Romans* 8:28

Many happy Valentine's greetings
to all of my readers. May love and friendship
abound for each of you.

Chapter One

An icy wind blew through the small town of Dry Creek, Montana, as Army Sergeant Mark Dakota pressed his black Stetson more securely on his head and braced himself with his metal cane. He was standing in front of the café and carefully leaned forward in hopes he could see through the window. Most of the glass was covered by a huge red poster advertising some Valentine event, but he could see around the sign well enough to know no one was inside the eatery. Except for his parked rental car, the street was empty.

The whole area looked deserted. Sitting on the wide-open plains of southeastern Montana, the scattering of buildings was eerily quiet despite the wind. Mark felt the same prickle of unease at the back of his neck that he'd had in Afghanistan several months ago, just before that roadside bomb exploded and tore his leg apart.

Suddenly, a dog barked and, without thinking, Mark threw himself to the ground.

"Uumph." He felt the resulting agonized jolt of pain all the way from his hip to his toes.

"That was a mistake," he muttered when he got his breath back. The doctors had cleared him to do routine physical activity, but this was over the line. He'd panicked.

Turning his head, Mark looked along the street and saw a brown mutt shoot out from behind a nearby house and come straight at him. By now, Mark knew that the dog's bark hadn't been a warning. This wasn't a war zone. Mark wore his civilian jeans and his old winter coat. Besides, the dog looked like a harmless stray.

"Easy, boy." The scruffy animal arrived and stood still. Then he eyed Mark, who was flat on the ground, carefully before crawling close enough to sniff at the soles of his worn boots.

"Good doggie," Mark murmured as he raised himself up slightly on an elbow and patted the dog, feeling along its spine until he was satisfied that the mutt was not starving. The animal might not be a family pet, but it was fed well enough.

Mark figured that getting a few scraps was about as much as any stray—man or animal—

could hope for in life. Using his cane, he struggled to his feet and watched the dog trot down the street again. That mutt reminded Mark of his place in life and he finally admitted to himself that he'd been a fool to come back here.

That letter his foster father Eli Rosen had written—the only one Mark had received from anyone in Dry Creek during the nine years he'd been in the army—demanded that he come home as quick as possible because Eli needed him. But Eli never needed anyone and, if he did, there was his real son, Junior. There probably wasn't any *brazen gold-digging woman* out to steal the Rosen Ranch either. As for the closing paragraph where he called Mark his son, the less said about that the better.

Still, Mark admitted, those final words from Eli had been enough to bring him back here just as surely as that dog returned to the households that occasionally gave him a bone. Mark stood, letting the pain in his leg recede while the air grew colder. Finally the distant sound of people singing "Amazing Grace" floated down the street. It was Saturday morning, not Sunday, but everyone must be in the church.

Well, there was nothing for it, Mark told himself as he squared his shoulders and began the long walk up the street. He couldn't turn back now without at least talking to his foster father. Given the growing wind, Mark was glad to reach his destination. The foyer of the church was dark and the doors from it to the inner sanctuary were closed. Mark let the warmth settle over him as he listened to the muffled sounds of what must be a prayer from the pulpit in the large room on the other side of the wall.

Suddenly, the double doors to the sanctuary burst open and two men in black suits stood there, looking shocked and staring at Mark. Bright sunlight streamed in from the windowed sanctuary behind them. He recognized the men; they used to work on the Rosen Ranch.

"Josh?" Mark asked softly. "Arnold?"

Arnold gave a strangled-sounding croak. "Mark? Is that you, son?"

Mark nodded, feeling more uncomfortable by the minute. By now, he saw they were holding the front part of a brass-accented coffin. It wasn't seemly for a funeral to have interruptions like this.

Suddenly, a small woman walked around the pallbearers and stood in the foyer, with what looked like a black choir robe billowing around her and a black blanket draped over her head like a shawl so that he couldn't see her face.

"Mark?" the figure finally spoke. Mark knew the voice well.

"Bailey? Bailey Morris? Is that you?" Mark hadn't shaved this morning. The color of his skin might betray his days in the Afghan sun, but his dark whiskers were all his own. Mark knew he looked unkempt.

The woman drew back the blanket and Mark could see it was his childhood friend. He recognized the flyaway red hair and emerald eyes that she'd had when they met in the first grade. Somehow though, the angles of her face had filled out since he'd seen her last. And her hair was slightly tamer and more styled. She'd be twenty-eight years old now. He took a second look.

"You seem—" Mark didn't know how to finish his sentence.

What had happened to dear old Bailey? She used to be comfortable in her appearance, like a favorite aunt sitting in front of the television in a tattered robe with her stockinged feet up and a bowl of popcorn on her stomach. Even with that black blanket, he could see this was no longer the Bailey he had known. Her skin used to be freckled something fierce, but now it was creamy with no hint of a spot. Her hair, carrot red for the decade he'd known her, was now auburn with dark blond streaks. Instead of frizz, she had soft curls. If he wasn't mistaken, she'd spent some real money at a beauty salon. That fact stopped him for a moment as he contemplated it. Bailey was beautiful—expensive beautiful. His whole world shifted on its axis.

"Did Gabe Rosen send for you?" she demanded to know, her words coming out low and her eyes sparking with fury.

That settled Mark's world back into place. She might be buffed up on the outside, but inside it was the same Bailey. She had been an outspoken seven-year-old when he had been sent to this community after the authorities tried, and failed, to track down his parents. He'd been abandoned in a gas station along the Dakota/Montana border. That's why the foster care system gave him the last name of Dakota. Bailey had decided mothering him was her right since she was an orphan, too, and in the foster care system like he was. When he protested, she informed him he was only six years old and couldn't know what awaited him in life. With her extra year, Bailey said, she had much more experience. She had sounded so sure that he'd believed her, at least for a few months.

Mark stood there, trying to figure out who could have died that would bring Bailey back to Dry Creek to pay her respects. Her elderly foster parents had passed away when she was in high school. Before Mark had left, she'd taken a good job working for an attorney in Los Angeles. She'd planned to go to law school at night and, in her words, *make a place for herself.* He wondered if she'd become a lawyer by now.

"Why would Gabe send for me?" Mark asked, picking on the point that made the least sense in all that she'd said. No one here knew he'd been wounded and was now on a medical leave while he decided whether or not to leave the army. No one, outside of Eli, would even know how to reach him.

The crowd behind the coffin must have parted, because someone stepped out. It was Gabe. He was a man now instead of a teenager, but he had the same lanky look to him. The son of Eli Rosen's cousin, Gabe had been a thorn in Mark's side when they were kids. The only good thing about having Gabe come for a visit to the ranch had been that Junior would align himself with Mark since they both thought Gabe was no fun. It was the only time Junior acted like he was Mark's brother and Mark had liked it.

"I'm protecting the old man's will," Gabe said with a look of determination that Mark had never seen on the man's face when they'd been boys. "Eli was like a father to me and I aim to see his wishes done. I saw a copy of the letter that he sent you," he said and glanced over at Mark before continuing. "I read what he said about a 'brazen gold-digging woman.' He apparently didn't want the ranch to go to Bailey and, no matter what she says or how she plans to twist the will, I don't believe he ever meant to give it to her."

"Bailey is the gold-digging woman?" Mark repeated in shock. Then he looked around. More people were crowding up to the pall-bearers so they could see what was going on. "That can't be right. Bailey might be controlling—maybe even a little bossy—"

"Hey," Bailey protested, her words no longer low or soft.

"But she's honest as the day is long," Mark concluded hastily. And she was too short to be a physical threat to anyone. "I'd trust her with my life."

Gabe snorted.

"And my wallet," Mark added so there was no question.

Bailey's face relaxed and she smiled.

Mark noted that the whole town of Dry Creek seemed to be buzzing and looking at him, Bailey and Gabe.

"Besides," Mark said, thinking this would

settle things, "doesn't Junior inherit everything?"

That made the whispering stop. Mark knew bloodline was important to Eli Rosen and that meant Junior, his only child, would be his heir. Pure and simple. When Mark first came to the ranch, he had been shown where his bed was in the bunkhouse with the hired hands and he'd been given his list of work to do. There had never been any suggestion that he move to the main house or become part of the Rosen family.

He found out later, just before he enlisted in the army, that the foster care people had no other place to put him except on the ranch. He'd been angry in those days and it showed. No one had wanted him in their home. The authorities must have thought the bunkhouse was a good compromise.

"From what I've heard the will might be complicated," Bailey said quietly as she backed up against the opposite wall of the foyer. "The reading happens after the—" She glanced back at the coffin.

"That's Eli, isn't it?" Mark whispered as he eyed the coffin. If he hadn't been so distracted by seeing Bailey, he would have figured that out from the pallbearers. Unsettled, he stepped closer to the foyer wall. "I didn't mean to interrupt."

The two ranch hands nodded.

"It's good you're here," Josh said, and the procession began again.

People passed by Mark, most of them giving him a smile and a curious look. Finally, only Bailey was left with him.

"I wish you didn't have to find out this way," she said as she walked over to him. "I know Eli could be a difficult man, but—" She paused, her eyes full of sympathy. She had always been able to pull the painful feelings out of him like they were nothing but meddlesome cockleburs caught on his shirttail.

They were both silent for a moment.

"Whether he wanted to be or not, he was the closest thing to a father I ever had," Mark finally admitted. It was pointless to confess that he'd had a flicker of hope when he first read that letter from Eli. The time was past for such dreams. "Eli was bigger than life. I never thought he would die."

Mark wasn't sure what a father was, but he knew it was more than just someone who lived, begat a child and died. He figured Eli must have known a secret that he hadn't thought to share. Junior had seemed satisfied with his father.

"I know what you mean about Eli," Bailey said. "I remember the time he gave us a whole roll of quarters so we could go on all the rides at the county fair. Just you and me."

"I was surprised," Mark recalled. He didn't think that gesture of Eli's revealed the secret of fatherhood, but it had been fun. "I'd never been as high as we were on that Ferris wheel."

"Or as sick as when we rode the whirly-twirly thing," Bailey added.

"You were only sick because you ate all that cotton candy," Mark scolded mildly. "That stuff will kill you."

"Not when you're ten years old," Bailey replied firmly. "It's all right then."

"Maybe," Mark agreed. He'd be the first to acknowledge that he knew nothing more about kids than he did about fathers.

They were quiet and then Bailey started to waddle away. Mark decided she was having even more trouble walking than he was. It had been a while since he'd seen a pregnant woman, but she sure seemed to be one. He wondered where her husband was, but he saw no one lurking in the door opening, waiting for her. Mark quickly put his hat on the rack by the door and extended his right arm to her. "Let me help you."

He gripped the cane firmly as she put her small hand on his other arm.

"Thank you," she said.

The cemetery was behind the church and that's where everyone was headed. Mark and Bailey walked slowly down the few steps going out of the building. The ground was gray and rocky, but, when they turned the corner of the church, they saw a large fenced square filled with flat name markers, a scattering of gravestones and even a few concrete angels. Plastic flowers were everywhere except where a new proper hole had been dug.

Mark didn't think Eli would be happy that his grave site looked so plain.

"I thought Junior would spring for a big marker of some kind," Mark said as he glanced around. He didn't want to show any disrespect to anyone. But he and Bailey were far enough behind the other mourners that they wouldn't be overheard. "Where is Junior anyway?"

Bailey's face flushed. "He's…ah, well—" She paused and didn't seem inclined to continue.

"What?"

Bailey stopped walking so Mark did, too.

"Junior isn't with us anymore," she finally said somberly.

"Took off on the rodeo circuit, did he?"

Mark whispered a guess as they started moving again. "He always said he'd do that someday."

Bailey shook her head. They were beside the open hole. She spoke in a low voice. "No, that's not it. He's dead. Car wreck. Alcohol. The usual."

By then they had caught up with everyone else and the minister was opening his Bible.

"We'll talk later," Bailey whispered as he stared at her.

Mark couldn't have said a word then anyway. Fortunately, the minister was saying everything that was proper. Dust did return to dust. The man cited the hope of heaven, but Mark figured that was just one of those nice things people said at funerals. He preferred to take death like a shot to the chin. There was nothing hopeful about it that he could see. As for the rest of it, God never had much time for him and Mark returned the favor.

Eli had at least written him a letter, Mark thought. Unfortunately, when it arrived, he was in the hospital trying to learn how to wiggle his toes again. When he'd left Dry Creek years ago, he hadn't thought he was saying his final goodbye to either Eli or Junior. At first, he told himself he'd come back when he became successful in life. He wanted their respect.

He'd thought about settling in Wyoming when he left the military. He'd seen ranches for sale on the internet there that were cheaper than those in Montana. Still, he planned to stay close to Southern Montana so he could travel to Dry Creek easily. For better or worse, this was his home and, despite the past, he hadn't been able to stop hoping that someday Eli and Junior would want him to be part of their family.

The cold air made Bailey wrap the blanket tighter around her shoulders. She couldn't believe Mark was here. Not after all these years. She tried to focus on Pastor Matthew Curtis as he spoke. She knew there was something she still needed to do but she was rattled and couldn't think of it. She watched as the pallbearers lowered the casket into the opening. She could still hardly believe that Eli had died. The old man had seemed immortal to her. Not that he had ever thought much of her; Junior had seen to that. But she had always hoped that a light bulb would go on inside Eli's mind one day and he would see that she had a good heart.

How had it all come to this?

She had loved Junior when she married him seven years ago, or, at least, she'd thought she did. Maybe it hadn't been a grand romance, but, right up to the day he died, she had intended to make a good home with him. That's all she ever wanted: to feel she had a place in the world. An orphan was too easily set aside and she never had felt the steady support of a family. She'd thought she'd find that by marrying Junior.

Pastor Matthew was reading the Twenty-Third Psalm, but the words flowed over her. Mark was standing beside her. She'd always thought that, if she saw him again, she would be wearing a designer suit and holding a leather briefcase. At first, she had thought a profession and a job would give her the grounding she needed. But when Junior had come to Los Angeles to visit her, she'd been homesick. Junior had promised her everything. It was like a whole new life was opening up.

She was glad Junior couldn't see her now. Between the scratchy wool blanket and the black choir robe that covered the only pair of slacks she could get into these days, she was a mess. Everyone in Dry Creek knew about her clothing crisis and would forgive her—she had, after all, taken the few clothes that still fit with her to the Salt Lake Hospital when Eli was transferred there to see a heart specialist.

They'd gone in a medical ambulance set up for the trip.

A few days ago, when she'd gone to the airport to come back to Dry Creek after Eli's death, she was told she couldn't fly because of her pregnancy. By that time her suitcase had already been checked in and couldn't be found. Finally, she learned it had been sent to New Orleans by mistake. By the time she got home in a rental car, her suitcase was still gone. If it wasn't for her five-year-old daughter, Rosie, she would have followed her suitcase and left the funeral to others.

Fortunately, a friend had stayed with Rosie while Bailey went to the hospital initially so her child was spared most of the pain of Eli's passing. That same friend had agreed to sit with Rosie during the funeral so Bailey could do her speaking parts in the service and then handle the flowers at the graveside.

That was what she'd forgotten, Bailey told herself as the minister said her name. "As the daughter-in-law and final caretaker of Eli Rosen, our Bailey Rosen will lay some flowers on the grave now," Pastor Matthew said.

Bailey had her hand on Mark's arm and she could feel his muscles tense at the use of her new name. He was no doubt surprised she'd married Junior. She'd never liked Junior that much in their childhood, but he'd seemed different in Los Angeles. That was in the past though, she told herself as she stepped forward.

Fortunately, she saw the white roses lying in a box beside the pastor.

"I object," Gabe spoke loudly before Bailey could even take a flower out of the box.

Everyone turned to look at him.

"You can't object," Bailey said firmly. "This isn't a wedding. No one gets to object at a funeral."

"That's true," the pastor agreed.

She wished Gabe had spoken out at her wedding to Junior instead of now, but the contrary man had just stood mute back then. And Gabe probably knew Junior wasn't one to stay faithful to any woman. Before Junior had gotten drunk and slammed his pickup into a concrete trestle, he'd already announced to everyone that he was going to divorce Bailey. She was not good enough for him, he'd said like he was some kind of a king. Plus, he added, he had a pregnant girlfriend in Missoula who needed him. Bailey hadn't bothered to tell him she was pregnant and needed him, too—or that she'd recently found out from one of his drinking buddies that Junior had yet another girlfriend in Bozeman who might or might not need him, as well.

That had been six months ago. She pushed thoughts of her dead husband away and reached down to the box of roses. None of that had been Eli's fault. She knew there were a dozen long stems and she picked up four to give to Gabe.

"Here. I'm sure Eli would like you to put a few on his casket."

Gabe looked at her dubiously, but didn't say anything as he took the flowers.

She picked up four more stems and also held them out. "Mark?"

Her old friend balanced himself on his cane as he reached for the roses. "Thanks."

She nodded. Together the three of them scattered the flowers over the top of the casket until the roses all lay there, their white petals mixing with the snow that was starting to fall.

Everyone was silent as dirt was shoveled into the grave.

"I didn't know he liked roses," Mark said quietly once the shovels stopped, a final blessing was said and people started turning to go back inside the church.

"I don't think he liked any flowers," Bailey confessed as she watched everyone leave but her, Mark and Gabe. "I just felt we should have some touches to show that people cared about him."

Mark searched her face. "You've been crying."

She shook her head.

"Your eyes are red," he persisted.

"It's probably the wool blanket. Itchy and allergies. My coat was in my suitcase," she paused and sighed. She didn't want anyone to know about her tears. "It's a long story."

Gabe looked over at her then and his eyes narrowed. "Pregnant women are always more emotional about everything. Those aren't real tears. Don't think you can sway that attorney."

"I'm not—" Bailey started to protest and then realized she didn't have much to say in her defense. She was at least eight months along and she did cry at odd times. "I'm not trying to influence anyone—at least not more than—"

Bailey stopped. She wanted some of that ranch and Gabe knew it. She needed to support Rosie and the baby that was coming.

"Not more than is fair," Bailey finally finished her statement. That much was true.

"We should get inside," Mark said.

Bailey wasn't deterred. She turned to Gabe. "You know that it's not unusual to be emotional at a funeral."

Then she turned to Mark. "The ladies of the

church prepared a luncheon for everyone." She glanced over at Gabe and nodded to include him, too. "I hope you will both join us."

"Of course, we will," Gabe said as though it was his right. "It's starting to snow and downstairs is the only place in town to get something to eat since the café is closed for the funeral. Besides, that attorney is reading the will to us after everyone leaves. I'm not leaving until then."

"I hope you won't try to sway him." Bailey threw the accusation back at Gabe as she turned and defiantly took the arm Mark offered. She'd thought it would make her feel better to shoot something back at Gabe, but it didn't. It just left her cold and damp.

"Don't be ridiculous," Gabe sputtered as she started to walk away. "I don't need anything from Eli. I'm a partner in a very successful law firm, for goodness sake. I'm not the one who needs a handout."

"I don't need a handout," Bailey turned and snapped back, no longer sorry she'd poked at him just seconds earlier. "I earn my way on the ranch. And I might go to law school someday myself. So there."

Bailey put her face forward again and started walking, leaning a little more on Mark's arm than she had earlier.

"I can't believe you married Junior," Mark muttered as they moved.

"Well, I did," Bailey said and then pressed her lips together so she wouldn't say anything else about that. She didn't want to whine about how unfair life was, especially not when it had been her own fault for thinking people changed.

"I didn't think you liked Junior that well," Mark persisted, sounding puzzled.

"It's complicated," Bailey answered, not looking up at Mark. At the end, she hadn't liked Junior. That's why she'd tried so hard to make him happy by looking her best all the time. She'd used facials to remove her freckles and had worn high heels around the house. She knew it made no sense. But she didn't want to tell all of that to Mark. She just needed to keep walking.

After Junior was killed, she realized she'd exhausted herself with all of her efforts. Marriage shouldn't be so hard. She figured that she just wasn't cut out to be a wife. She supposed it was best to find that fact out in her twenties rather than to be miserable with some other man in the future. She had Rosie and the coming baby. That was enough family for her. She'd silently pledged to herself never to worry about a husband again.

She looked up at Mark as they came to the doors of the church. He'd left his hat inside and the wind was blowing his black hair. Snowflakes had settled on his forehead. He was handsome and he looked like he could move mountains with just a shrug of his muscled shoulders. It was too bad he knew even less about marriage and family life than she did. Besides, he probably expected women to spend their lives parading around on high heels, too.

"I'm never getting married again," she announced.

"But you have to," he protested, looking a little shocked. "You have a baby coming."

"Being married or not won't change that fact," she said. "Not at this date."

She'd forgotten that Mark could get indignant if family things weren't done just so. He thought every child needed both parents, but especially a father. Fortunately though, he didn't press her further.

She wondered where his army career had taken him. He likely had a girlfriend in every port around the world by now. His blue eyes would tempt most women to thoughts of romance. His body would do the rest. Of course, she supposed, it was not the ports, but every military base since he was in the army and not the navy. Either way, he was off-limits for her.

Chapter Two

Mark wished he was wearing his army uniform with those pressed seams and golden chevrons instead of his old ranch clothes that had spent the last six years in the bottom of his trunk. Bailey had insisted he and Gabe stand with her in the receiving line just inside the church basement. Gabe was in a dark gray suit that looked tailored and Mark didn't like being shown up in the wardrobe department by a childhood irritant who was now a loud-mouthed lawyer.

"I should have at least shaved," he muttered to himself. No one heard him though. There was enough chatter going on to hide the explosion of a small bomb. At least he had that to hold over Gabe, Mark thought. He knew how to defuse most kinds of small bombs. Gabe would probably just let the thing explode.

Feeling better, Mark looked around. The day outside was overcast and, even though it was early afternoon, only a faint light came in through the high narrow windows of the basement. The beige walls were painted concrete. Fluorescent lights hung from the ceiling. Long folding tables, with white plastic covers, filled the middle of the room. The smell of coffee was in the background and he'd guess that beverage would be perked the old-fashioned way. Aproned women, carrying dishes of all sizes, scurried between the main table and the small kitchen.

It all felt homey. The only bad part, in Mark's opinion, was that there were still plenty of people waiting to shake the hands of those few people who had any remote claim to being Eli's family.

"You remember Josh Spenser?" Bailey turned to Mark as the hired hand stood in front of them both. "He was one of the pallbearers and he used to work on the ranch."

Josh held his hand out to Mark and he shook it firmly. The man's hair was as black as Mark's, but his cheeks were clean-shaven. Dark brows furrowed over his green eyes as he looked at Mark cautiously. Josh was two years older than him, and had come to the Rosen Ranch under some kind of federal work program for ex-prisoners. "Of course, I remember," Mark said, doing his best to be cordial as he faced the man. Mark was going to make some comment on the passing of time but then it hit him what Bailey had said. "You used to work there? I always thought you'd stay at the ranch forever. What happened? Find a better job?"

Mark could see that had been the wrong thing to say. The man's face flushed red and his eyes swung back and forth between Mark and Bailey until he looked like he was guilty of something. Mark wondered if the man had been fired, although he couldn't see Eli doing that. Josh had worked hard.

"Leaving was the thing to do," Josh finally muttered. "A man's got his reputation to think about—and the reputations of others, too."

By then the next ranch hand was there.

"Arnold Green," Bailey said curtly. The smile she'd worn was gone.

Mark scrambled for something benign to say to the older man. "Nice suit you have on."

Arnold, who had to be in his fifties now, looked at Mark with relief and nodded. "It's a rental. Josh and I got a good deal since I work at the tuxedo store in Miles City now."

Arnold held out his hand. Mark shook it willingly and smiled, stopping himself from asking any more troubling questions. He couldn't imagine Arnold being in a clothing store for most of the day. The man used to complain about being cooped up in the barn during spring calving. And he certainly didn't know anything about fashion. He didn't even bother to match his socks.

Both men moved on to Gabe. No one was standing in front of Mark then so he could clearly hear the nearby conversation. He told himself he shouldn't listen, but he couldn't stop his ears from doing their job as Gabe smiled, gripping each man's outstretched hand in turn. "I think Eli knew neither one of you was to blame."

Mark turned in surprise. "Blame for what?"

Josh and Arnold had been loyal hands. He couldn't see them making an unforgivable mistake. Maybe one of them had burned down the barn. He recalled Arnold smoking a cigar now and then.

Gabe looked at Mark and then jerked his head in Bailey's direction. Mark changed his gaze to where Gabe indicated. Bailey had her head down and a woman in a black floral dress had shifted to talk to the person behind her in line, thus giving Bailey a moment to herself. Bailey looked miserable.

"What's wrong?" Mark asked her softly.

She looked up and he saw the tears shining in her eyes. "Don't worry. You weren't even around here. I don't think they can blame you either."

"Blame me for what?" he whispered.

"For my baby," Bailey said softly. "As bad as Junior talked about me at the end, some people don't believe he's the father of this child I'm carrying. They think I was having an affair, only they can't figure out who it would be with. I never even saw any men except at church and then Josh and Arnold. They're both single, too, which made it worse. Especially for Josh since he's more my age."

"Oh." Mark wished he was back in Afghanistan taking incoming fire. Gossip was the problem. "I can't believe anyone would think that who knows you. These people must be new."

"They are," Bailey admitted. "And they don't know me. They were Junior's drinking buddies."

"Then people won't credit them. I wouldn't worry too much about what they think."

"You'd worry if you lived here," Bailey said, her head coming up and her words starting to gather fire. "You'd worry if you were going to raise your daughter and baby here."

"Daughter?"

"Yes, my daughter, Rosie. She's not to blame for any of this either."

"Of course not." Mark was glad to see Bailey was showing some spirit again.

The woman who had held up the line turned around and he recognized her with gratitude. She always seemed to show up at the right time. It was Mrs. Edith Hargrove, the feisty woman who had taught Sunday school to the youngest Dry Creek children for the past fifty years. Both Bailey and he had been in her class when they first moved here. If anyone could sort everything out, gossip included, it was Mrs. Hargrove. She wasn't afraid of anyone, certainly not of men who drank too much and told lies.

"Mark Dakota," Mrs. Hargrove said, greeting him. Her voice was raspier than he remembered, but her cheeks were still pink and her white hair was pulled back into her usual sensible bun. The black floral dress, that looked like it was made out of silk, was quite a bit fancier than the gingham dresses that were her standard wear. Mark peeked down and noted that her orthopedic shoes were the same style she'd worn when he had been in her class almost twenty years ago.

He took her hand and smiled at her. "It's a real pleasure to see you again."

"Thank you. And I'm sorry about Eli. He'll be missed. And I know he always relied on you."

Mark respected that she hadn't said Eli had loved him or even held him in special regard. It was true the man had relied on him to do a variety of chores. That much Mark could accept as his due.

Mrs. Hargrove had a firm grip for a woman who must be in her eighties, Mark thought as he nodded at her words. She was the heart of this community. It was good to see some things didn't change.

Just then Mrs. Hargrove moved and he saw a young slip of a girl hiding behind the older woman's dress. The girl looked to be around five years old and she wore a simple gray dress with a wide white collar. Pearl barrettes held her curly red hair behind her ears. She stared up at Mark shyly, turning her head a little as though measuring him.

Mrs. Hargrove was still talking to Bailey, but the girl stepped out of the folds of the older woman's skirt and faced Mark.

"I'm Rosie," she whispered and pointed at Bailey. "That's my mama."

Mark nodded. So this was the daughter. "You have a nice mama."

She smiled and then was silent for a bit. "I don't have a daddy no more though."

"I'm sorry," Mark muttered, relieved that she didn't look like she was going to cry or anything. He wished he had a piece of hard candy in his pockets; that's what he gave new recruits when they had a shock.

"He died," Rosie added, not sounding upset at all. "And he got to go to heaven."

Mark needed rescuing. He looked around for someone to help, but Bailey and Mrs. Hargrove were locked in some conversation. He heard the phrase *Bible study* so he didn't want to interrupt them. He turned to his other side and saw Gabe was talking with someone, too.

Mark finally looked back down at the girl.

"Heaven is—ah—nice," he carefully said. Surely, the idea of heaven was good. He wasn't opposed to it in any event. "I hear people want to go there."

That much was true.

He looked down and noted a faint frown on the girl's face. She seemed to be concentrating.

"You have a cane," she finally said. He didn't remember Bailey ever making small talk, but that must be what her daughter was doing.

"The cane's nice and shiny," he agreed, glad they were back on safe ground. He lifted the cane a little and gave it a twirl. "It works good, too."

He tapped the cane on the floor for a little extra emphasis.

A look of satisfaction flashed across the girl's face and she nodded.

"You had a hat, too," she said as she looked around. "Where did it go?"

"I put my hat on the coatrack in the foyer," he answered. If he was able, he would have bent down so he was on her level. He thought he'd read somewhere that children liked that. And, even with all the questions, he wanted her to stay. He did lean over a little just to be sociable.

"I suppose you like cowboy hats," he said, making a special effort to keep his voice soft. She seemed fragile and he still wasn't sure she wouldn't start crying.

She shrugged. "I thought it might be a top hat." She sounded disappointed.

Just then Bailey looked down and seemed to notice who her daughter was talking to. Bailey reached out to pull the girl back.

"We'll be finished with the line in a minute," Bailey said to Rosie. "Only a few people left. Then I'll fix a plate for you and we can sit down and have some lunch. Would you like that?"

Rosie nodded. "Can the man with the cane eat with us, too?"

The girl was looking directly at him, Mark noticed, so he took the liberty of nodding his head at her. "I'd love to—"

"You don't need to," Bailey moved closer and whispered. "She's only interested in your cane."

"I don't see why—" Mark began.

"It's the Valentine youth talent contest at the café," Bailey informed him. "She wants to find someone with a cane and top hat to be her partner in a tap dance number. It's even better if they can sing."

"Like Shirley Temple," Rosie nodded in confirmation, her eyes gleaming with excitement before turning to her mother. "He doesn't have a top hat though."

Bailey looked up at him and was going to speak.

"Oh, I'm sorry," Mark said, before she could say anything. "I don't think I could dance—I mean, even if I had a top hat, I—"

Mark watched the light fade from the girl's eyes. She had likely never heard of knee reconstruction. He glanced over at Bailey and saw she didn't look happy either.

"I could maybe find you a top hat though," Mark offered impulsively. All he would need to do would be to go online to a party store. "And someone could borrow my cane. Then all you'll need is a partner."

The girl's shoulders slumped down. She had burrowed into Mrs. Hargrove's dress and he could barely see her face.

"No one wants to be my partner," Rosie whispered finally, the sound so low Mark wasn't sure he'd heard her correctly.

"Oh, I'm sure—" Mark began to say but a cutting look from Bailey stopped him.

"I told you I can be your partner," Bailey said cheerfully as she reached over with her hand and brushed her daughter's hair off her forehead. "We'll tap a duo."

"But—" Rosie lifted her eyes to her mother, but Bailey had already turned to greet the last couple in the line.

Rosie turned to Mark instead and whispered, "Mama can't dance. She's got the baby inside her. And the contest is only two weeks away."

"Wars have been won in two weeks," Mark answered with the most encouraging thing he could think to say.

Rosie looked thoughtful. "Do they tap dance in wars?"

Mark shook his head. "But they do reveille every morning when they wake up. Not in active war so much, but… That's where the trumpet blows and the troops salute."

"Can you play the trumpet?" Rosie asked him hopefully.

"No, sorry." Mark felt particularly useless. "I can salute though."

He demonstrated and the girl smiled so he

clicked his heels together, too. It didn't hurt as much as he expected and she looked pleased.

Finally, Bailey came to his rescue. The line of people was gone now. "We need to go up front. Everyone is waiting for us to get the first plates so everyone can eat."

Rosie took a step toward Mark. Then she held up her hand for him. "I'll show you the way," she said in a matter-of-fact voice as he took her offered hand.

"You don't want to get lost," Rosie said as they stepped forward. "You'd be hungry."

Mark had a sudden need to blink. Not that a tear was forming, he assured himself. It was just the damp of the basement getting to him. He gratefully sat where the girl indicated he should. He'd never had a child worry about him since Bailey had years ago. Strange that he should suddenly miss it.

The smell of a dozen homemade casseroles filled the air as Bailey sat down in a folding chair that Mark had pulled out for her. He gave her his arm to lean on as she seated herself at the table. Then he sat back down next to her in the chair Rosie had assigned him earlier.

"My daughter is usually very shy with strangers," Bailey said as she looked at Mark suspiciously. The girl had already flitted away to get them napkins. Rosie said she was worried the ones with the pink flowers on them would be all gone by the time Bailey and Mark could get their plates filled.

"I think she's still hoping I'll help her with the talent show," Mark responded ruefully. "I would, but I'd move stiffly even if I tried. And I can't sing."

"You could wear the hat," Bailey said, teasing him a little.

"That I could do," he agreed.

"Don't worry," she assured him. "I'll be able to move enough to help her."

Mark looked at her skeptically, but he didn't comment further.

Bailey gathered the choir robe more closely around her. She had found a white butcher's apron to go over the robe and she looked more normal. She noticed Pastor Matthew go stand near the kitchen door.

"The pastor will say a blessing for our food," one of the kitchen ladies announced in a loud voice. The chatter ceased.

Everyone bowed their heads and the pastor thanked God and the ladies for all the food. He also asked for comfort for Eli's family and friends.

When the heads were raised, Bailey and

Mark were motioned to come to the head of the line. Bailey noted that it was Mark who gestured for Gabe to join them while she called Rosie over to take her hand.

Bailey hadn't realized how hungry she had been until she took a bite of two local dishes. Mrs. Hargrove's daughter Doris June made her usual halibut bake and Linda Enger, the café owner, made green chicken enchiladas. Bailey followed those dishes with Mrs. Hargrove's buttermilk biscuits.

"This is good," Mark whispered on her right, a note of reverence in his voice. "I haven't eaten like this since—" he stopped for a minute "—why, I guess since I left Dry Creek years ago. It certainly beats anything in the military."

Bailey nodded. There would be no shortage of words of condolence, but the good people of Dry Creek always did practical things to help a family who was mourning. She suspected they would try to send most of the leftovers home with them and she'd have many offers to take Rosie for an afternoon of play. She was glad. Even though she and Rosie had been living there for several years, Eli's ranch house would seem very cold without him around.

Dessert was served before Bailey quite realized it and the lawyer, who had driven out from Billings, had arrived, brushing snow off of his wool coat. Bailey was surprised a young woman was with him. She was tall, but hunched her shoulders like she was trying to take up less space in the world. Bailey thought she was probably a teenager, but she might be older.

"Feel free to get something to eat," Bailey said as she walked over to greet the lawyer. She turned to the almost-woman. "And your daughter, too."

"I'm not his daughter," the female said, her voice flat. She sent the lawyer a look that made Bailey wonder even more who she was. Maybe the man had picked up a hitchhiker, Bailey thought. As she looked closer, the woman seemed like she'd fallen on hard times. Everything she wore was frayed. She wasn't dressed much better than Bailey was in her choir robe. Suddenly, Bailey saw why—the woman, and she supposed she had to be old enough to be one, was as pregnant as Bailey was.

"Nothing fits, does it?" Bailey said sympathetically. "But you should eat. You need your strength."

"I didn't come here to eat," the stranger said and turned her back on Bailey. When she stood tall like she was, her frame, apart from the bulge of her pregnancy, was alarmingly thin.

"Oh," Bailey said as she looked up at the lawyer. He'd taken off his coat and laid it over a folding chair. His suit was what she figured a power suit must be. It was dark gray with thin black stripes going through it. He wore a dark red tie and carried a genuine leather briefcase that gave Bailey a pang of envy. That's what her briefcase was supposed to look like someday.

"I think we'd better just start," the lawyer said. "I understand there is a small room where we can meet. There will be five of us—Mark Dakota and Gabe Rosen will be included, too."

"Yes, of course," Bailey said as she gestured to a classroom. It was Mrs. Hargrove's Sunday school room, but it was the largest of the side areas. Bailey had already set up a few folding chairs for the meeting. "I'll get more chairs for us."

Mrs. Hargrove had agreed to keep an eye on Rosie during the meeting.

It was Mark who brought in the extra chairs and Bailey was glad for it. She was beginning to have a bad feeling about that tall woman. She had noticed a ragged red University of Montana T-shirt under the bulky gray sweater that she wore. The University of Montana was in Missoula.

"The T-shirt. Are you a student there?" Bailey addressed the question to the woman's back.

She didn't turn around. "Thrift store find. I plan to enroll next year."

"Still in high school?" Bailey asked.

"I'll be twenty-one soon. High school is a long time ago."

"Oh," Bailey said as she sat in one of the chairs. Mark sat next to her. Finally, everyone was seated.

The lawyer opened his briefcase and brought out five copies of a legal document.

"The will," the lawyer announced, keeping all of the copies in his hand. "I'll go over the main points and then you can read them for yourselves. I'll take any questions at the end."

Bailey thought she might faint. She reached out and took Mark's hand. He gave hers a gentle squeeze.

"Just keep breathing," he whispered to her.

Then the lawyer began speaking again.

"First, Eli wanted me to say that he values his family very highly." The lawyer paused and looked directly at each person there. "But he wants to be sure that his family is his family by direct descent. Bloodline only."

Okay, Bailey told herself as the lawyer looked at her. Eli had heard the rumors. She knew that much already. He'd wondered about her baby, too.

"Eli is willing to give up to one hundred percent of his ranch and all the assets, less those he specifies in this will, to you, Junior's legal wife," the lawyer said as he looked at Bailey. "If the baby you are carrying is a boy and is shown, through medical tests, to be the offspring of Junior Rosen—"

Bailey gasped. "What if my baby is a girl?"

"If your child is female," the lawyer continued, "and is shown to be the offspring of Junior Rosen, and no other confirmed offspring is found then you will receive the full amount."

Bailey almost stood up, but the lawyer didn't stop.

"If your child is female," he said, "And there is another verified offspring, male or female, then the assets will be shared equally."

Bailey sat down as Mark's grip on her hand tightened.

"What other child?" Bailey asked, her voice faint now that she suspected what was coming.

The lawyer gestured to the young woman who'd come into the basement with him and was sitting beside him. "Miss Emma Smitt is—"

"I told you I am Mrs. Junior Rosen," the

woman interrupted. "I have the marriage papers right here."

The woman had pulled some papers out of a pocket.

"I explained that those are not legal," the lawyer said, pity in his eyes.

"But we got married," Emma protested. She looked a little desperate.

"Junior was already married," the attorney said patiently. "He couldn't legally marry anyone else. And that minister who said the words over you wasn't even licensed. I'm sorry, but—"

"Junior told me we were married," Emma said, looking at the whole room. "I never would have—you know—I told him we had to wait and we did."

Bailey felt sorry for the woman.

"He told his father about us," Emma insisted further.

Bailey wondered if this was Eli's gold digger. It gave her comfort to think that Eli might have not felt that badly about her.

"How far along are you?" Bailey asked and Emma looked over at her.

"A little over seven months," the woman whispered and put her hand on her stomach. "I didn't even know Junior had died in that accident until the lawyer drove up to the mountains and told me. Junior told me he'd be gone for some months because he was riding rodeo to make enough money to give us a good start when the baby came. He couldn't call me because I don't have a phone. My trailer doesn't have cell coverage anyway. It's out a ways."

Bailey knew enough to know it wasn't rodeo season.

"Do you need help?" Bailey asked, suddenly realizing the girl might be more desperate than she'd thought. "Do you have any neighbors close that can help? I don't have much, but—"

The girl straightened her back. "I get by. Junior left me with groceries. And I have a pickup. And Tommy Two, of course. He's good company."

Bailey was glad the woman had someone, whoever Tommy Two was. Right now Emma looked pale enough that she really might pass out.

"Let me go get her something to eat," Bailey said to the lawyer. "I'll be right back."

The lawyer nodded and Bailey stood up.

"Let me go with you," Mark said.

Together they went out into the rest of the basement. The women were all in the kitchen. A few men loitered around the edge of the room. Only the dessert table had any food dishes left on it.

"These will do," Bailey said as she picked up a plate piled with iced ginger cookies.

After they got back to the room, Bailey passed the plate around and insisted Emma take two cookies. She noticed the woman's hands shook as she reached for them.

"I'll get you a sandwich later," Bailey said. Then she looked at the lawyer. "Let's finish this."

The lawyer nodded. "I'll make it brief since a storm is coming in. Assuming Bailey's baby is fathered by Junior, if it's a boy and he survives, she inherits half. If her baby is a girl and both her baby and Emma's baby survive and are Junior's, then things will be split fairly evenly. I can be more specific later."

"What about Rosie?" Bailey asked. "She's Junior's daughter."

"I'm afraid Eli didn't factor her into the percentages," the lawyer said with a grimace. "I mentioned her and Eli said he knew she was Junior's. But hc's more interested in any male heirs that Junior might have. Again, those percentages will be after the other two bequests are honored."

Bailey's head was spinning. She wasn't quite sure about the conditions and percentages but she'd wait to read the document itself. "What are those?"

"The first one is thirty thousand dollars to Mark Dakota," the lawyer said. "Whenever Mark is able to collect it, which is now, thankfully." The lawyer looked at Mark and smiled. "Good to see you again, son."

Mark nodded and Bailey realized the lawyer must have met Mark years ago on the ranch.

The lawyer shifted and continued, "Eli figured most of it as back pay for the years Mark worked on his ranch without compensation. The rest is to pay for Mark to help out on the ranch until both babies are born and the will is applied."

Mark inhaled and his grasp of her hand weakened.

"I can't believe he's paying me for those years," Mark murmured. "He never thought he owed me."

"I think his conscience was bothering him on that point," the lawyer said. "Eli wanted to make things right when he died. He knew you were due regular hired hand wages, especially in your teenage years. You were a hard worker, he said."

Everyone was silent at that.

"What was the other bequest?" Bailey finally asked.

The lawyer looked at Gabe now as he spoke. "Eli is giving a hundred thousand dollars to build the bell tower for the Dry Creek church. He wants Gabe to oversee the project." The lawyer raised an eyebrow at Gabe. "In fact, that's a condition of the bequest, I'm afraid, you have to handle it or it doesn't happen."

"Of course, I'll do anything," Gabe responded. "Eli was the only family I had left after my father died."

The lawyer nodded. "You'll be paid ten thousand dollars for administrating this. Eli wants you to get hold of the Amber Cast Iron company and hire them. One of the regrets Eli said he had in his life was the way he treated this company when they came to Dry Creek a decade or so ago to build that very bell tower."

Bailey felt her stomach flutter and she looked over at Gabe. His face had gone pale. They both remembered that time.

"Eli had a big argument with them," Gabe said. "Yelled at the father and insulted the daughter. I didn't know what it was about, but I was there shortly after the words were said. She was crying. It was so bad. She was only twelve or thirteen. They might not be willing to come back."

"You'll have to convince them if you want that church bell tower," the lawyer said. "You're authorized to offer them more money if needed, but you're not permitted to find a different company. They probably wouldn't want to start until spring or summer anyway so there's some time to think about it. I have a sealed envelope that Eli left for you about this. You need to come to my office and sign for it in front of a notary. Other than that, I know you can offer them a cruise or something if they don't agree at first. Sort of a signing bonus. Find out what they might want and make it happen."

Gabe nodded. "I'll try."

Bailey noticed Gabe didn't look very happy about his task. It struck her that none of them were going to be pleased with this will—except for, maybe, Mark. She glanced over at him. He was stoic. She never had been able to read him when he was upset. She didn't know if he'd planned to stay in Dry Creek for any length of time at all.

Bailey turned to Mark and asked, "Can you do this with your army duties?"

He nodded. "I'm pretty flexible right now."

"That covers the high points then," the lawyer said as he started to pass out the copies of the will. "There is more in the document about percentages and who gets what in what scenario. Call me if you have any questions. I think Emma and I better get back before the roads start to ice over."

"You don't have someone on your list who is from Bozeman, do you?" Bailey asked anxiously.

The lawyer shook his head and seemed to know what question she was asking. "That young lady was not—ah—in trouble."

Emma eyed Bailey. "Who's that you're asking about?"

"No one—not really." Bailey saw no reason to add to the other woman's grief. She wondered if Emma still loved Junior.

Everyone sat still for a bit and then the lawyer and Emma both stood and started to walk out of the room.

"Wait, let me get you those sandwiches," Bailey said, but when she started to rise, Mark gently pressed her to stay seated.

"I'll get them," Mark said as he rose.

"I'll help you," Gabe said.

Together, the two men left the room following the lawyer and the young woman who thought she'd been married to Junior and had no idea that the man who she thought had married her already had another wife and a spare girlfriend.

Bailey sat there looking around at the artwork the preschool students had made. Bold strokes of crayon formed trees and mountains and more than one sun. She wished life was that easy to depict.

"You really messed up, Junior, didn't you?" Bailey whispered to the walls. "You lied to that woman. And you've got us all twisted up in it."

Bailey felt sorry for herself, but she felt even sorrier for Emma.

Bailey listened to the footsteps of the lawyer until it sounded like the man was at the door leading up to the main floor of the church. She couldn't hear Emma's footsteps. She thought the young woman was wearing sneakers. She was likely walking right along with the lawyer, just taking silent steps.

Then Mark poked his head into the room. "They're gone."

"And they have a sandwich with them?" Bailey asked.

"Two hearty meatloaf sandwiches each," Mark said. "And a few apples, as well. Mrs. Hargrove put everything in two brown paper bags. I think she snuck in a small carton of milk for Emma, too. She used big bags."

Bailey nodded. "Thanks."

"Mrs. Hargrove says the rest of the food goes with you and Rosie," Mark said. "She's packing it up now."

Bailey looked up. "And you? You'll come with us, won't you? Gabe is staying in the room over Mrs. Hargrove's garage so there's no available rooms in town, but the bunkhouse is empty now so there's plenty of room out at the ranch."

Mark nodded. "I guess that's what Eli wanted so I may as well get myself settled there."

"We can read over that will and figure it out better later," Bailey said. "I'm not sure I got it all."

"First thing tomorrow," Mark said.

"Tomorrow's Sunday," Bailey said. "Rosie and I go to church."

"Then the first thing tomorrow afternoon," Mark said. "And I think you could use a nap this afternoon, too. It's already been a long day."

Bailey smiled as she stood up. "The longest."

Together they walked out into the main room.

Bailey knew she hadn't pressed Mark on going to church. She was only coming to a timid faith of her own. She'd have to talk to him about it. Maybe after her nap. Right now, she was tired. Not that she was likely going to be able to sleep with thoughts of that will in her mind. At least Mark was here. She felt better just remembering that.

Chapter Three

A couple of hours later, Mark stood on the steps of the bunkhouse and looked out at the Rosen Ranch. It was starting to grow dark. He had his winter coat on and he'd found a pair of work gloves in the nightstand beside his old bed. Even in the poor light, he could see that the whole place had been neglected. Everything here used to be in fine shape. Sometimes when he hadn't been able to go to sleep in the military, he'd remember every detail of this ranch. He'd always assumed Junior was taking care of it.

Now, even with the light snow covering everything, he could see the scars that came from lack of attention. The corrals by the barn had a rail lying on the ground, likely rotting in the damp. A cow must have rubbed against it on some hot summer day, scratching her back until the nails loosened. No one had fixed it and eventually the rail had fallen down. The barn itself needed painting. A metal garage had been added between the barn and the house. The field behind the structure was filled with nothing but dead weeds. It didn't look like a crop had even been planted last fall. A plow certainly hadn't turned over any of the ground.

And, thinking of cows, Mark had only seen two. The others might be out in the back fields, but he wondered who was feeding them this time of year. They'd need hay. He wondered if Eli had given up on raising cattle. Most ranches here focused on growing wheat, but he saw no evidence of that either. Josh and Arnold must have been gone since late last summer. The absence of any signs of occupancy in the bunkhouse meant no one had replaced them.

Mark started to walk out to the barn. He had always liked ranch work. In fact, he'd saved his pay for the past six years hoping he'd have enough to put a down payment on a small ranch when he left the military. He hadn't had quite enough when his leg had been blown apart, but with the thirty thousand dollars Eli was giving him, he should have enough. He'd work his two or so months here at the ranch and look around for a likely place to buy.

He was still officially in the army on medical leave, but before he left Afghanistan, he'd started the process for a discharge. Unless he pulled the plug in a few weeks, it would go through. If he stayed in the army, it would mean a desk job and he didn't want that.

For the first time, the timing for all of this felt right to him. If he had a ranch in this neighborhood, he could keep an eye on Bailey and Rosie. That realization cheered him up considerably. He'd be here for the new little one, too. From the sounds of it, Bailey didn't have any plans to get married right away again so he'd have some time with them before another man came on the scene.

He frowned at that thought. Bailey hadn't shown much sense so far when it came to picking a husband. He definitely should stay and give her some guidance. Make sure she found a solid man this time. He didn't like the thought of her hooking up again with someone like Junior.

Just then he heard the grinding gears of an overworked engine. He looked back and saw an old pickup turn in to the Rosen Ranch lane. The driver had to shift down as the vehicle headed right up to the main buildings.

Mark guessed it was some rancher's wife who had not been able to get her casserole to the church on time and was now dropping it off for the family. He didn't know how they would eat all the food they'd already been given, but he knew the drill. He'd smile and thank the woman profusely. They all needed the good-will of their neighbors more than they needed food.

The pickup window was open and he saw at once that the driver wasn't a woman.

The vehicle came to a stop and Josh Spenser stepped out. He'd changed out of the suit he'd worn earlier and was in range clothes that looked a lot like the faded ones Mark was wearing.

"Good to see you," Mark greeted the man as he held out his hand to Josh. "Thanks again for carrying the coffin today."

"It was an honor," Josh said as he took Mark's hand. "Eli was always a fair-minded boss."

Mark grunted. "He was a hard, demanding boss. He didn't pay a penny more than he had to."

"Yeah, well," Josh said, his lips curving up slightly. "I grew up here, but when I got out of prison he hired me when no one else would have. I didn't have a very good attitude back then. I owe him for that."

Mark nodded. He wasn't about to ask any

more questions of either of the ranch hands. "I'm guessing you're here to see Bailey."

"No," Josh said, looking nervous. "At least, I wanted to see you first."

"Oh?" Mark said, trying to sound encouraging.

"I got to thinking," Josh said. "Since you're back and all, there might be a need for another hired hand on the place."

Mark grinned. "You mean now that you don't have to be here with just Bailey?"

Josh looked sheepish. "You know how folks love to gossip."

Mark nodded. "Yeah, I do."

"Besides, I'm tired of staying with my uncle and his family," Josh said. "The bunkhouse looks pretty good about now. It's at least quiet."

"I'd be all in favor of working with you again," Mark said. "But I think the decision is Bailey's—at least for now. The will apparently gave her some expense money for the ranch."

"It wouldn't need to be much," Josh said. "She could owe me some of it until everything is settled."

"Speaking of the ranch," Mark said. "Do you know where the cows are? Eli surely didn't sell them all, did he?"

"They're at Durham's place. In that section bordering our far pasture," Josh said. "Durham has been feeding them from the haystack over there. He doesn't cotton to it much though, especially with his rheumatism and all the snow this year. In fact, he's been talking of retiring. I'm guessing Eli had to pay a pretty penny to get him to do the job. It's cold as blazes some mornings."

"We could bring the cows down to the section behind the barn," Mark said. "Might need to fix some fences, but calving will be in full swing soon and we need them close anyway."

"Durham would be relieved and we would save money," Josh agreed. "I check on the cows when I drive over that way—just on my own like—and they look lonesome. Sometimes I give them a holler and they come over to see me. I think they'd like to come home."

Mark considered that statement for a moment. Women liked that kind of sensitivity. They were all about fixing lonesome beings. He took a long look at Josh. The man might have possibilities. He'd come a long way in the past few years.

"Well, let's go ask Bailey about all this," Mark said as he started toward the house. She had wanted him to wake her up about now anyway if Rosie hadn't already done so.

"How have you been doing?" Mark asked as they walked together across the frozen ground.

"I don't have a job."

Mark nodded. "I mean, in your—ah—personal life."

Josh shook his head. "I'm trying to figure my life out actually. Quitting my job here made me realize I need a better plan than just working for someone else forever."

Mark stopped and faced the other man. Not only was Josh sensitive, he was strong and moderately handsome. Sounded like he had ambition, too. Mark looked a little closer. The man's hair had been blown around in the wind, but it was straight and shiny black. It went good with his green eyes. He even had a dimple. Of course, Josh had a suspicious look on his face now that they were standing out here in the cold talking about things men never even whispered about normally.

"Why?" Josh asked finally. "Worried if I'm up for the job?"

"You don't have any illnesses, do you?" Mark questioned. He needed to press on. "Problems with the heart, feet, teeth—that sort of thing."

"Not a thing."

"No genetic problems."

"Not that I know of."

"Good," Mark said. He felt relieved. "You've got lots of work years ahead of you then."

They stood there silently, looking at each other.

"I was never asked these questions when I applied to work here before—not even with my time in prison," Josh finally said, a slight frown on his face. "I don't think it's really legal, you know."

Mark looked close to see if the man seemed upset. He didn't—at least not much.

"Just thinking a man your age should be looking to his future—like you said," Mark replied, trying to sound casual. He rolled his shoulders to relieve the tension there. "I suppose you have a girlfriend."

Josh shook his head slowly. "No—not to speak of."

"Okay," Mark said as he started walking again. "Good."

Mark realized that setting Bailey up with a new husband was going to be more difficult than he thought. Maybe he needed a written questionnaire. That was what they would do in the army. He knew he couldn't assign someone to the task, but it didn't hurt to know which recruits were available.

Bailey was hanging up the telephone when she heard footsteps on the porch. The airlines had called to say they would deliver her suitcase to the back door of the café in Dry Creek tomorrow morning before nine o'clock. Since the café was closed, no one would see it until she came. Finally, she thought, she'd be presentable when she went someplace. She could change in the restroom at the church before the service.

"I'll get it, Mommy," Rosie said before Bailey even heard the knock on the front door.

"Wait for me," Bailey called out as she hurried over to catch her daughter. If it wasn't for the pickup she'd heard a few minutes ago, she would assume it was Mark at the door. Even at that, though, she didn't want Rosie answering any doors unless she knew for 100 percent sure who it was.

"It's Markie!" Rosie squealed in delight as Bailey opened the door.

"His name is Mark, sweetie," Bailey said as she placed a hand on Rosie's shoulder to keep her from spinning around. "Either that or Mr. Dakota."

"Oh," Rosie said, looking at the floor.

"I'll answer to Markie," the man said as he stood there in the open door, looking impossibly handsome, Bailey thought. It must be her hormones going into overdrive with the baby. The collar of his coat was up and snow had gathered on his Stetson. He had shaved since she saw him earlier. He also looked like he was on a mission. She remembered that expression on his face from their childhood. He was up to something.

"Well, then, please, come in," Bailey said, opening the door wider and only then seeing there was another man with Mark.

"Josh!" she exclaimed in genuine pleasure. "I had no idea you were here."

Bailey stepped aside so she wasn't blocking the doorway. "Both of you come in where it's warm."

Mark stepped inside and then Josh did the same. Both of them stood huddled on the rug in front of the door.

"I don't want to get your floor wet," Josh finally said.

Mark nodded, beaming. "He's well trained. Knows about housework and all."

A look passed between the two men that she didn't understand.

"I'm not applying to be a maid," Josh said curtly.

"No, of course not," Mark said. "Being tidy never hurt anyone though. The army requires it."

"Well, I appreciate you sparing the floors," Bailey said as she stepped over to a small closet and pulled out two folding chairs.

"These will do," she said as she set them up.

One on each side of the rug, so the men could sit to take off their boots.

Soon, the door was shut against the cold and two pairs of men's boots were sitting on the top of the rug.

A few minutes more and all four of them—Bailey, Rosie, Mark and Josh—were seated at the old red Formica table in the kitchen with cups of hot chocolate in front of them. Eli had installed a bright light over that table and Bailey was grateful for it. The rest of the kitchen was in shadows now.

"I hope you'll stay and eat with us," Bailey said to Josh after they'd finished the cocoa. "We have enough enchiladas and Mexican rice to feed an army."

"I'd be happy to…" he replied, hesitating for a moment and then continuing. "The fact is that I came over to ask if you'd want to take me on as a hired hand again. I know the job and the cows know me. I would save you training someone else. And, if you check around, you know I put in a good day's work at whatever I set my hand to doing."

"I'd certainly vouch for him," Mark added when there was a pause.

"There's no question about you being a good hand," Bailey said. "I'm just not sure about paying someone—"

"You could owe me until the will is figured out," Josh said. "Give me room and board and I'm happy to wait for the full amount."

"Well, then, welcome back," Bailey said with a grin. "I hated looking at that bunkhouse when I knew it was empty. Oh," she suddenly realized. "That place must be as dusty as anything. It's been months since anyone has even swept the floor out there. And the sheets!" Bailey started to rise. "I'll need to wash the sheets for two of the bunks. Or does one of you want to stay in the foreman's suite?"

Bailey had almost forgotten the large room and private bath that were traditionally set aside for the man who used to direct a large number of hired hands. If she remembered right, there was a small refrigerator and galley kitchen with it. There might still be a couple of rocking chairs and a small sofa.

"You just sit tight," Mark said as he stood up. "I'll go gather up the sheets and bring them in here. We'll wash them while we eat."

"I'll go help, too," Rosie declared as she slid down from her chair.

"It's too cold," Bailey protested. "And dark."

"Markie can take me," Rosie insisted.

"I will if you can hang around my neck like you're riding a horse," Mark said. "You'll have to put your legs around my middle and hold on tight. I have to use my one arm for the cane."

"There's no need for that," Josh said as he stood up. "I can go over and get the sheets."

"No, no," Mark said. "You stay here and keep Bailey company. Tell her how those cows are missing the home place."

There was that expression on Mark's face again, Bailey thought. She couldn't imagine what he was plotting though unless… *That's it*, she thought. *He's worried about me walking on the snow when I'm this pregnant.* Well, he did have a point.

It didn't take long for Rosie to be hanging on Mark's neck with his coat covering them both and buttoned up. She saw Rosie lay her head down on the back of Mark's shoulder and smile quietly to herself. Before she knew it, the two of them were out the door and stepping into the darkness. She stood there for a moment and heard a fake horse's neigh and a girlish giggle when they were a few yards away from the house.

She closed the door and went to the refrigerator to pull out what she would warm up for dinner. As she worked, putting everything into the oven, Josh dutifully told her about the cows who wanted to come home. She was only half listening because it had occurred to her as she brought out some broccoli salad that Rosie was in danger of becoming too attached to her Markie.

Fortunately, she forgot about her concerns when Mark brought an armload of sheets back and needed instructions on how to use the washing machine.

"Honestly, I'm happy to do it," Bailey said after her second trip to the mudroom off the kitchen.

"No, I can do it," Mark said as he studied the buttons. "I just need to know what to push when."

After the sheets were ready to take back to the bunkhouse and dinner was over, everyone decided to make it an early night. Josh and Mark left.

Bailey was grateful as she took Rosie to her room and started to get her ready for bed.

"Mommy," Rosie said as she put her arms through her nightgown.

"Yes, sweetie," Bailey said.

"What do daddies do?" Rosie turned as she pulled the nightgown down and looked at Bailey.

Bailey wasn't prepared for that. She supposed she should have been.

"Why do you ask?" she said, keeping her voice calm.

"Do they give their kids horsie rides?" Rosie asked.

"Sometimes," Bailey said. "And sometimes they read a bedtime story. Or they make sure their child has brushed their teeth before they go to bed."

Bailey was keenly aware that Junior had done none of those things.

"But mommies can do all those things, too," Bailey said, keeping her voice positive. "A little girl doesn't need a daddy for those things."

"Oh," Rosie said, thinking a moment, and then climbing into her bed.

"Do you want a bedtime story?" Bailey asked, feeling like she should give her daughter more. She pulled the covers up and tucked them in so Rosie was warm.

She shook her head. "I'll just go to sleep."

"Okay, sweetie," Bailey said as she stood up and went to the door.

Bailey turned off the light in Rosie's room and went back into the kitchen. That room was still warm and held the sense of people having just left.

She walked over to the window over the sink and saw the light burning in the bunkhouse. She had a feeling she and Rosie were both going to have a hard time with Mark being here. They needed him, no question about that.

But he might only stay for a few months. It wouldn't do to get too close. She didn't want Rosie hurt. Bailey decided she should talk to Mark tomorrow after church.

She suddenly wondered if he would even go to church. He never had once he'd become a teenager and Eli gave him a choice. She guessed she'd find out. She would need to share her own faith with him soon. Now that he was back at the ranch, it would be natural to tell him everything that had happened to her.

Chapter Four

Clouds filled the east as the sun fought to break through, sending streaks of golden pink across the rim of the sky. It was seven fifteen in the morning and Mark stood at the front door of the ranch house. Dressed in the same clothes he'd worn yesterday, he was warm enough. He looked down and noted that the tip of his cane was covered in mud. Yesterday's snow had started to melt. It was going to be a cold, wet day, but likely it wouldn't be freezing.

"Bailey," he called out softly. She had told him to come over about now to make coffee if he wanted an early cup. He reached out, putting his hand on the doorknob. Bailey said the house would be unlocked, but it held firm.

Mark rubbed his face and felt his whiskers. He intended to shave before he put on a clean shirt, but he didn't have a razor. Of course, he didn't have a clean shirt either. Josh had said last night that past hired hands had left an assortment of shaving kits and shirts around. The bunkhouse was pretty empty, but Josh said some of those things were probably stored in the closet off the laundry room next to the kitchen.

Mark heard a door close inside the house so he knocked lightly. He didn't hear anything else and he was beginning to think no one had heard him. He raised his hand to try again when he saw the curtains on a side window move.

Rosie's little face appeared for a moment. Then the curtains fell back into place. She must have raced to the door because the lock disengaged and she opened the door much sooner than he expected.

"Markie!" she cooed in delight. She wore pink pajamas with gray elephants all over them. "It's you."

She made it sound like he was the grand prize of the day.

"What are you doing up with nothing on your feet?" Mark asked as he stepped inside the living room. He didn't want to scold her, but the alternative was to stand there grinning like a fool. No one had ever thought he was a prize before.

"I lost my socks," she replied cheerfully.

"Aren't your toes cold?" Mark said as he closed the door.

Rosie looked down at her feet and nodded. Then she lifted her arms up to him. "Carry me."

"I'm colder than the floor," Mark said as he leaned on his cane to slide his wet boots off. "And damp all over. Maybe I can set you in a chair and put a blanket around you." Mark grabbed a knitted afghan from the nearby sofa. He'd put on thick socks when he'd dressed earlier and he was grateful for them as he walked back to the girl.

He scooped Rosie up in one arm and carried her to the kitchen, setting her on a chair and wrapping the cover around her until she was snug. Looking around in the morning light, he saw the walls were a faded yellow. Last night they had looked beige. The red Formica table was the same though. It was bare except for a pair of salt and pepper shakers. The side wall had a tractor calendar and the old rounded refrigerator by the sink had a dozen magnets on it. This was a working ranch kitchen. The only thing missing was a coffeepot.

"Is your mother up?" Mark whispered.

Rosie nodded vigorously and spoke softly. "She said a bad word." Rosie paused and then added primly. "I'm not supposed to hear bad words."

Mark heard the indignant gasp before he turned and saw Bailey standing in the doorway between the hall and the kitchen. She had a hairbrush in one hand and she was wearing an old blue-and-gray flannel robe with a tie closure caught in her other hand. Her green eyes were snapping and her auburn hair was flying all around. Mark thought she was beautiful.

"I have not been saying any bad words," Bailey announced firmly.

Mark put his hands up in a gesture of surrender.

But Rosie looked at her mother and wrapped the afghan around her ears. "It's okay—I don't hear."

"I said I look a mess," Bailey continued, eyeing her daughter. "That's not a bad word."

Rosie studied her mother and then dropped the cover away from her ears, but Mark didn't think she was convinced.

"When I'm a mess you say it's bad," Rosie argued.

"Well, no one likes a mess," Bailey admitted. "But it still is not a bad word."

Rosie didn't say anything.

Mark reminded himself to watch his language around the little girl. She was sharp.

He noticed that Bailey looked over at him and cinched the robe tighter above her stomach.

"I thought I'd be up by now and have some breakfast ready for you," she said to him. "I always try to fix a hot breakfast before we head out to church. That way we can concentrate better on the sermon. If you just give me a minute, I'll—"

"Don't rush on my account," Mark said. "I'm perfectly able to fix breakfast and I'm not planning to go to church. I haven't been in ten years."

"Oh," Bailey said.

She suddenly looked so tired that Mark rushed to pull out a chair from the table. "Here."

Bailey sat down.

Rosie crawled down from her chair and went to lean her head against her mother's shoulder. "You're not a mess—you're my mama."

Bailey reached out an arm to embrace her daughter. "Thank you, sweetie."

Then she looked down at her daughter. "Where's your socks?"

Rosie shrugged. "I lost them in my bed."

"Well, you can't be walking around on these chilly floors in your bare feet," Bailey said.

"Markie can be my horse," Rosie offered hopefully.

"Absolutely not," Bailey said. She turned and glared at Mark like he wanted to be a horse. "You're not to encourage her. She's got two good legs and she can use them."

Mark grinned. Bailey was looking more like her normal self now. "I'll just set her back on her chair and tuck that afghan around her. No horsie, I promise."

Bailey nodded. Then she braced her hands on the table like she was going to get up. "I'll get the coffee going."

"You just sit tight," Mark said as he plucked Rosie up and set her on her chair. "I can find my way around the kitchen if you point me in the right direction. I'll get the coffee going. Then maybe I'll make us a bunch of pancakes and some scrambled eggs."

Bailey opened her mouth and Mark thought she was going to protest, but she finally closed it. "I don't know when the last time was that someone made breakfast for me."

"I'm surprised Junior didn't do it," Mark said until he thought a moment and realized the other man would never do that. "Anyway, I'm glad to do it."

"We usually have the flakes," Rosie said from her chair. "With milk."

"Sometimes I make oatmeal," Bailey added and then hung her head. "That's what Eli likes—I mean liked. Oatmeal with raisins and brown sugar."

Mark was thankful he knew how to make pancakes and eggs. He thought Bailey was on the verge of tears. "Just sit there and rest a bit more. You'll need your strength for going to church."

Bailey obeyed for once.

"I suppose they have coffee at the church like they used to." Mark realized he was chatting away, hoping to keep Bailey's mind off Eli. Everything was silent for a minute and then he heard a deep sigh.

"You're right," Bailey said. "Everyone at church will know about the will by now. Even Mr. Clemens will know and he says he won't go inside that church even if someone pays him a million dollars."

"So how's he going to hear about the will?" Mark asked as he opened a cabinet door. He didn't know any Mr. Clemens.

"Someone always talks," Bailey said, looking even more discouraged than before. "And people stop at the Clemens house to complain about his pit bull. He's got it fenced in, but it's scary and the fence isn't that good."

Mark reached up to a top shelf and pulled the coffeepot down. "I don't see what it matters if people know about the will anyway—oh," he stopped. "You're worried they're going to know about Emma."

"Of course," Bailey said, almost glaring at him. "And they're going to know that Eli wasn't any too sure that my baby is really Junior's child. For one thing, Gabe has a standing invitation to come here for Sunday dinner. He'll be at church. He'll spread the word."

"And come here afterward?"

Bailey nodded with a bleak look on her face. "He's family."

Mark took another look around the homey kitchen. Like he'd noticed earlier, it wasn't a showcase place; ranchers and their families had lived in this house for over eighty years. It had its share of nicks and scars. But he'd guess that more than one problem had been solved around the table where Bailey and Rosie sat.

"Maybe you should stay home this morning," Mark said as he began to fill the coffeepot with water. "I'm sure everyone will understand. I think Josh is going to the services. He can tell folks that you're tired."

"But I have to go," Bailey said as she stood

up. "I'd rather answer the gossip today than let it go for next week."

Mark watched as she took a minute to find her balance. She was one brave woman. "I guess I'll go then, too."

He had no choice, he told himself. He'd go into battle with any of his troops who were facing enemy fire. Bailey needed him. He wondered if she went to both Sunday school and church services. He hadn't been in either since he was twelve years old and Eli said he could decide about going. He hoped the church would remain intact and not be struck by lightning just because he showed up. He remembered some of those Old Testament stories from Sunday school. Fire and brimstone were the norm. He wondered if there was any hope God might not recognize him. His looks had changed a lot since he'd been twelve.

Bailey twisted the black choir robe around her as she hung up her old ranch coat in the foyer. Josh had driven in earlier with his pickup and was likely already seated in a pew. She, Rosie and Mark were late and she hadn't had time to stop at the café and pick up her suitcase. She knew it would be waiting at the back door of the eatery when church was over. She could hear Doris June start to play the piano inside the sanctuary so everyone was probably getting settled.

"It's time," Bailey said softly as she reached down and took Rosie's hand. Then she looked up at Mark. "Thanks for coming."

He gave her a curt nod and she knew he was nervous. He'd shaved after breakfast and had found a white shirt in that closet off the laundry room. She thought it had belonged to a ranch hand that had left years ago. Mark had ironed the shirt, but it was tight on him and still looked like a thrift store special.

"You look good," Bailey said as he offered her his arm. He'd taken care to pick a white shirt, after all. That had style even if the garment didn't have any starch to it and was missing several buttons. She saw one safety pin put to good use.

"I'll need to get a few new shirts," he admitted. "Next week."

She nodded.

Mark opened the door to the sanctuary and the three of them walked midway down the aisle to a pew that had room for all of them. A hymn was called and the singing of it helped calm Bailey. She loved being in church with her spiritual brothers and sisters, even on a day like today when she felt they might not understand her situation.

The words of the sermon soothed her, but she could feel Mark fidget beside her.

Lord, be with my friend, she prayed quickly. The pastor was explaining that believers were meant to help each other. She knew Mark prided himself on being a loner. At least that had been his way as a child.

Bailey glanced over to where Gabe sat and tried to think of words to bless him. God said to pray for our enemies and she tried to do so. She couldn't think of words, but vowed to give it some thought in the afternoon. She knew Gabe was going to be lonesome without Eli. That alone made her sympathetic.

The closing hymn came too soon to please Bailey. They had only sung one verse of it when the doors to the sanctuary slammed open and a dog started to howl.

"What's going on?" Bailey said along with the whole congregation as they turned in unison and stared at the back of the church. The temperature went down twenty degrees and the scent of wet dog slowly filled the air.

Mr. Clemens stood at the edge of the doorway into the sanctuary. The outside doors were wide open behind him. Technically, she supposed he was not in the church proper since neither toe of his worn boots had crossed the strip that separated the tile of the foyer from the inside carpet. Not that it looked like the man cared about that or anything else. His long gray hair was damp and scraggly. He had a bruise on one side of his face. His wet khaki-green coat, likely purchased at the army surplus store in Miles City, was open and a dirty white T-shirt showed through. He wore old sweatpants that were tied with a fraying string.

"It must be raining," someone in the congregation muttered.

"I know that dog," Mark said, low enough so only Bailey heard.

"What's wrong, Mr. Clemens?" the pastor asked, his voice louder than the others because he still held the microphone in his hand.

"It's this blasted dog," the old man practically yelled as he held up the rope that was clearly meant to restrain the dog. The animal whined pathetically as the noose tightened around its thin neck. "This confounded stray has been running around like an outlaw on his way to everlasting perdition."

Bailey looked down and saw Rosie reach up and cover her ears.

"It's a killer dog," Mr. Clemens continued, his voice growing louder now that everyone was listening to him. "It almost killed my Lulu."

"He almost killed who?" someone whispered.

Bailey didn't know any Lulu.

"Who's Lulu?" Rosie looked up and asked. Bailey noted that her daughter must not have covered her ears very tightly.

"Is she little like me?" Rosie questioned and Bailey reached over and gathered her daughter closer to her side. The girl was afraid.

"No one will hurt you while I'm around," Bailey said to her daughter.

"Do we need to take Lulu to the clinic in Miles City?" the pastor asked, concern deep in his voice. "You came to the right place. We can ask for a couple of volunteers right now. Is Lulu unconscious?"

"Of course not," Mr. Clemens retorted. "She's just lying there licking herself where this beast bit her."

Everyone was silent at that news.

"Mr. Clemens," the pastor finally asked. "Is Lulu your dog?"

"Of course she's my dog," Mr. Clemens said. "What did you think?"

"It's just that you always call your dog *my pit bull*. I didn't know it had a name," the pastor commented.

Mr. Clemens seemed a little quieter. "That's true enough. She's a purebred, you know. I paid good money for her when she was a pup. I'm proud she's a pit bull and I like for folks to know it."

Everyone was wordless and then the pastor spoke again. "So she's all right, except for the bite?"

"It's a crime that she was bitten," Mr. Clemens persisted. "And if the goody-two-shoes in this church hadn't been feeding this worthless stray, he'd have left this area weeks ago."

"But where would the dog have gone?" the pastor asked. "We can surely open our hearts to one homeless dog."

"It's a killer beast and I want it strung up and hung," the old man said defiantly as he reached into the pocket of his jacket and pulled out an ancient pistol. "Either that or shot in the head until dead."

Bailey gathered Rosie even closer and noticed that Mark had stepped nearer to both of them, too.

"Get down under the pew," Bailey whispered to Rosie.

"Is he going to say bad words?" Rosie asked as she started to kneel.

"I don't know," Bailey said softly. Mr. Clemens didn't look well and the pastor didn't seem to know what to say.

"Please, Lord," Bailey whispered. She saw several others with their heads bowed.

Not everyone was praying though. Mark

was slipping past her and stepping out into the aisle.

"Say, Mr. Clemens," Mark said in a friendly voice. "Do you mind if I take a look at that gun of yours? Do you know the year it was made? I used to have an old Colt revolver. Looked something like yours. I'm guessing you got it at the army surplus store. Is that still going in Miles City? Off—what was the street again?"

By the time the questions were over, Mark had taken the gun from Mr. Clemens and Bailey started to breathe again.

"I don't have any bullets in it," the old man confessed as Mark passed the gun off to the pastor.

"You still scared folks," Mark said and then he stepped aside as Deputy Sheriff Carl Wall came rushing into the church. Mark remembered him from when the lawman used to visit the Rosen Ranch. Carl usually attended services, but today he must have been doing something else. Obviously, someone had called him on a cell phone.

It took a few minutes, but the deputy finally escorted Mr. Clemens outside.

"Think he'll go to jail?" Mark asked Bailey when he came back to the pew.

"I don't know," Bailey said. "Deputy Wall might let him stay in his house and take care of his dog until the judge calls him in. Mr. Clemens wouldn't have any place to go and Carl works with people when he can."

Words of relief spilled out from the congregation once someone said Deputy Wall had Mr. Clemens in his patrol car and was talking to him.

A few people started walking down the aisle when suddenly all of them stopped.

The low sounds of a dog growling reverberated throughout the sanctuary. Bailey realized that the dog hadn't moved from his place in the doorway even though the old man had.

A few of the people scurried back to their pews and Bailey could see the stray animal standing there almost daring anyone to come near him. No one could get past it to the foyer.

"That dog has gone bad," someone whispered.

"What are we going to do about it?" another woman asked aloud.

"It really doesn't belong here," a man answered. "Not if it's terrorizing good folks and biting their pets."

"I'd hardly call that pit bull a pet," someone else opined. "And it was old man Clemens who scared everyone."

"Well, I'm going to stop feeding that stray, that's for sure," a final voice stated.

"Nobody needs to feed it any longer," Mark declared as he stepped back out into the aisle. "I'm taking it home with me."

Mark started walking toward the mutt.

"Be careful," a woman cautioned Mark. "That dog is wild."

"Catch hold of that rope first," a man added. "Or use your cane to keep it back."

Mark went straight up to the dog and offered it a hand to be sniffed. The stray lay down on the floor and rolled over. Mark obliged by scratching its stomach.

Bailey had never been prouder of her friend.

The rest of the congregation looked sheepish.

"I never meant I wouldn't feed it at all," the woman who'd spoken up earlier said. "Just not so much."

Usually, the ladies only served coffee between Sunday school and church, but today someone had the coffee perking and people stayed in the foyer talking and drinking a cup. They were probably trying to steady their nerves.

"Your young man is quite handy to have around," one woman said as she gave Bailey and then Rosie each hugs.

"He's not my—" Bailey replied. "He's just a friend."

Mark had taken the dog outside. Bailey looked over and saw the small smile on Mrs. Hargrove's face.

Then loud voices came from the steps in front of the church.

"What in the world?" Bailey exclaimed and joined the line of women streaming through the open doors. The day was not warm, but it wasn't as cold as she expected. The sun was shining a little. There was still more mud than dry ground outside though.

Mark was standing at the bottom of the stairs with his cane, the growling dog at his side, and a half dozen men milling around. From the looks of it, Bailey figured the quarrel hadn't been decided.

"You can't mean to take that dog out where we have our herds," one man, a rancher who Bailey knew, challenged Mark. "He'll be trouble. Just look at him."

Bailey had to admit the dog looked fierce.

"If he's trouble, then he's my trouble," Mark answered calmly.

Bailey knew it would be her headache, too, but she didn't want to interrupt. Who would take care of the dog when Mark left? She had to think of things like that.

"You know that's not the end of it," another

man said, entering the fray. He obviously took a long view of things, too, Bailey thought.

The man continued. "Fences don't hold a dog back. You can tell he doesn't like having us around. How are you going to stop him from attacking someone else's animals? I have horses. And goats. You'd have to run like the wind to catch that dog before he nipped at a mare's legs. He could maim an animal permanently."

All of the men looked at Mark's cane.

"I'll train him," Mark replied, more steel in his voice than earlier.

"Only a tenderfoot would take a chance like that," another rancher said. "I say we take him to the vet and have him put under. Be done with it."

"He's a healthy dog," Mark protested. "Bothering no one."

Bailey agreed with that.

"He's a killer," another man said. "Just like Mr. Clemens said. What kind of a mutt takes on a pit bull?"

"One that is defending himself," Mark countered. "Haven't any of you ever been on the other side of things and needed somebody's help?"

No one spoke. Bailey squeezed her lips together so she wouldn't say anything. She and

Mark knew what it was like to be unwanted and in need of help. They had been just like that poor animal.

"I say again that you're a fool to take in that dog," one of the men finally said.

By that time the women were lined up and down the front steps of the church. A few of them still wore aprons under their coats. Bailey noted that Mrs. Hargrove was at the top of the stairs.

"And I say he's a hero," Mrs. Hargrove pronounced loud and clear as she walked over to the handrail and started down the steps. "It's not wrong to save a life."

Most of the critics at the bottom of the stairs were looking slightly ashamed. Bailey knew their children were taught by Mrs. Hargrove. Some of them might have been in the older woman's Bible class themselves. She was the conscience of the town.

"It's only a dog," one of them muttered.

"And in God's eyes, we're nothing but lumps of clay," the older woman countered as she kept climbing down. Moving slowly, but with purpose. "Think about that before you harm a creature of His."

Bailey watched until Mrs. Hargrove reached the ground and stood next to Mark. Then Bailey started down herself.

"You always were a hero as a boy," Mrs. Hargrove said as she put her hand on Mark's arm. She continued in a softer voice. "You were brave, but I used to worry if it was for the best."

Bailey knew that when Mark first came to Dry Creek, this woman opened her arms to him and loved him. Mark never seemed to completely accept it, but he must have known he had her support.

"What do you mean?" Mark asked cautiously.

Mrs. Hargrove answered in what was almost a whisper, "You always mean well, but I wonder if being a hero is only your way of keeping other people at arm's length." She paused and added. "You offer protection, but not yourself."

Mark didn't say anything.

"Is there anyone you're close to?" the older woman asked quietly.

By now, Bailey was at the bottom of the steps and she saw the stricken look on Mark's face. No one else was watching, but she was.

"I'm close to people," Mark protested, his voice almost a whisper. "Lots of people."

Bailey took another step toward them.

"Are you sure?" Mrs. Hargrove asked that question so softly that Bailey knew no one but she and Mark could even hear it.

"Of course, I—" Mark started and then stopped, looking trapped even though everyone but the three of them was already moving away from the church. Most people were almost at their vehicles on the street. No one else saw him.

Bailey felt Mark's eyes concentrate on her face. She was only a few feet from him now and Rosie was trailing behind her.

Suddenly, Mark closed the distance between them and bent down.

Bailey saw his face coming and, feeling startled, turned to see him more clearly. She didn't know what he was doing.

His cold lips met hers with determination. The shock of it kept her still for a moment. She knew he'd been aiming for her forehead and she'd unwittingly made him miss by tilting her head. But now they were kissing for real and she could not move. She felt rooted to the ground. Finally, the cold feeling turned warm and the pressure became a gentle coaxing. Bailey felt a rush of longing race through her and she couldn't seem to stop it for the longest time. Her heart was filled with regret for what wasn't and wouldn't be.

Bailey finally realized that people were fluttering and chattering around her. Most of them must have turned around minutes ago and walked back to protect her. She wondered how long she'd been lost in thought.

"Well, I never," one woman said, her voice carrying through the still morning.

Bailey agreed with that sentiment. She'd never either. Finally, she stepped back and stared up at Mark. The man didn't look like he was caught up in the moment. Instead, he seemed to be hiding behind a wall.

"I was making a point," he finally muttered. She thought he would say more, but he didn't.

Bailey took a moment to digest those words.

"You were making a point!" Her voice was weak, but she drew herself up to her full height even though she still didn't come up to the middle button on that shirt of his. "I don't think anyone should be kissing anyone just to make a point."

A murmur of assent swept through the people around them.

"You're quite right, Bailey," a woman called out.

Mark's face looked frozen again. She had no idea what he was thinking.

"I'm sorry," he finally said formally and turned. "Josh already said he'd give you and Rosie a ride back to the ranch. Or you can go out with Gabe. I don't want that dog around Rosie until we know how he'll handle himself."

With that, Mark led the animal over to the ranch pickup. From what little Bailey could see she assumed he settled the mutt on the floor of the passenger side. Then she saw him walk around the cab and climb in on the driver's side.

By that time, everyone else except her, Rosie and Mrs. Hargrove were gone. Even Josh was waiting in his pickup. She couldn't see where Gabe was. Hopefully, he'd already left. Maybe a few others had, too.

"Well, that was a—" Bailey started to say a *mess*, and looked down at her daughter, stopping herself. "A disaster."

"Maybe not," Mrs. Hargrove answered cheerfully.

"What would you call it then?" Bailey asked, her voice not as polite as she would like. "I don't know anyone who wants to be kissed so someone can make a point to the world."

Mrs. Hargrove grinned. "He wasn't worried about proving something to the rest of us. He was proving it to himself."

"Really?" Bailey had her doubts.

Her old Sunday school teacher nodded with that wise look she often had. "I'd call it progress."

Bailey didn't have an answer for that. She knew hope and faith were rock-bottom certainties in Mrs. Hargrove's life. Bailey had no desire to challenge Mark Dakota. He shouldn't be kissing her for any reason at all. She was eight months pregnant and she had troubles enough with that and Eli's will. No man should be kissing her now. She'd have to make that clear to Mark.

Chapter Five

Mark kept his eyes focused on the gravel road. The sun was shining steady and the air was warming. Wisps of clouds showed off a blue sky. Straight ahead, he saw field after field that had patches of dirt and dried weeds emerging from the melting snow. Barbed wire cut the land up into squares. Ranching had always struck Mark as pretty organized. Except, he thought, when animals were involved. They were the wild card.

He looked down at the dog. It did something to a man to be responsible for an animal, he thought. He'd talk to Josh about moving the cattle back to the Rosen Ranch on Monday. The cows needed looking after. He wished he and Josh could move them this afternoon, but it was Sunday. That had always been a day of rest in Eli's time. He supposed it was futile to hope things had changed.

Mark wished he didn't have to go back to the Rosen Ranch, but Sunday dinner would be mighty slim if he didn't. The café was closed. The pumps at the gas station on the edge of town would be open, but the inner office would be locked. He thought there was a vending machine next to the building, but it might be empty. He'd be fortunate if he could buy a pack of stale crackers. "I played the fool," he said softly as he glanced down at the dog. No, not *the* dog, he told himself, it was *his* dog. "I don't know why I thought I could come back here and mingle with regular people and everything would be okay."

He hadn't fit in here as a growing boy. He didn't know what made him think it would be any different now. He'd done fine in the army. He'd known what was expected of him. Nobody cared why he was a hero or if he cared deeply about anyone else. Not even the doctors putting his leg back together asked those kinds of questions.

"Maybe the army is where I belong," Mark said, feeling a little depressed at the thought. He'd have to notify them if he wanted to stay in the service.

His dog whined. Mark looked down at the

mutt. The animal had a pained expression on its face.

"You understand, don't you, partner?" Mark asked, feeling better.

The dog yipped twice, increasing in volume each time.

"Oh," Mark said as he brought the pickup to a halt. Maybe the pained expression wasn't for his situation. "I should have thought of that."

Mark stepped out of the cab and walked around to the passenger side. He opened the door and the mutt jumped out. Mark kept the animal on its makeshift leash, but he let him move around until he found a place to do his business.

Within minutes, Mark and his dog were on their way again.

When they turned off the gravel road onto the dirt lane that led to the bunkhouse, Mark searched to see if there were any signs that someone else had beaten him back here from church. He knew Gabe parked his car right in front of the main house and it wasn't there. Josh, however, could slip his pickup into several places. Often the other man parked on the side of the barn. It didn't look like Josh was home yet either.

Mark could see a distant vehicle coming

down the gravel road he had just traveled. "I might try the barn myself."

Mark hadn't had a chance to look inside the barn since he'd been back, but he suspected there would be a place where he could fix a bed for his dog. The mutt hadn't seemed to like being in churches so Mark wasn't sure how it would react to a house. The barn would certainly have an animal smell to it and that might appeal to his guest.

The barn's roof consisted of rough handmade shingles and several of them were missing, letting streams of light inside in various places. Mark knew he'd have to get up on that roof and fix them during the next dry spell. A line of stalls filled the far end of the barn. A tack room opened off the side and bales of hay were clustered beside the wide main door—the one that allowed a tractor and wagon to be driven inside to load or unload feed.

By the time Josh's pickup pulled up to the house, Mark had a stall outfitted for his dog.

"It's for your own protection," Mark said, reassuring the mutt as he coaxed it into the enclosure. "I don't want you running around until the neighbors know you mean no harm."

Mark put the final blocking board in place as Josh stepped through the barn door. The man must have walked over from the house.

He was in the shadows at first, but then he moved slightly and his white shirt stood out.

"Need any help?" Josh asked as he looked around. He had on a new black Stetson and a silver-plated belt buckle. "That dog hasn't bitten you or anything, has he?"

Mark shook his head. "He's more frightened than anything. Most any animal will fight back when attacked. And he was up against a pit bull."

"I reckon that's so," Josh said as he walked over to the stall and leaned over to see the dog. "Just so you know, Rosie wants to come out here. That's all she talked about on the ride home. She calls him *the poor little doggie*."

Mark grinned. "That girl would take up for a full-grown wildcat if she felt sorry for it. I'll have to see how it goes though." He considered it a minute. His dog was quiet. "I guess she could come see him now that he can't get to her. Maybe after we eat. The dog is acting pretty tame."

Josh nodded and was quiet for a moment. Then he turned to face Mark.

"Just so you know," Josh added, sounding reluctant. "Bailey doesn't seem to want to come out here, dog or no dog. She's..." He paused. "Upset, I think."

Mark didn't know what to say to that so he

let the comment go unanswered even though he knew Josh was studying him.

Josh finally cleared his throat. "Did you really kiss Bailey?" His words were abrupt, like he was exploding with curiosity. "I didn't see it, but I heard it was a smacker."

"Heard it from whom?" Mark asked, trying to keep his voice even. Bailey seemed particularly upset with gossip.

"Everybody," Josh answered. "The guys at the hardware store. Even the women. I don't think the children knew. Unless maybe some of the older ones."

Mark's teeth clenched and he had to slowly relax them. "Sometimes a kiss isn't what it looks like."

"How's that?" Josh asked, looking sincerely interested.

"Sometimes in the battlefield, men do strange things," Mark replied. He didn't know where that came from, even though it was true. Some things a man just couldn't explain. He wished everyone would just ignore that kiss.

"Oh, it was the gun," Josh replied, relief evident in his voice. "That makes sense. I'm sure that old gun of Mr. Clemens's brought back memories of war for you. Sort of like post-traumatic stress."

Mark looked up in surprise.

"I wouldn't say that," Mark said, although he didn't know what he would say. None of the doctors had suggested he had post-traumatic stress. They'd asked a few questions, but mostly they had just focused on putting his leg back together.

As Mark stood there he became aware Josh was watching him, probably looking for anything like twitches or tics that would prove his theory. Mark was glad the man hadn't seen him fall to the ground earlier over a dog barking.

Suddenly, Mark heard the sound of another vehicle driving up the lane.

"That will be Gabe," Josh said and leaned closer. "Don't worry. I'll explain to him about the PTSD. We don't want anyone giving you a hard time."

"You don't need to do that—" Mark started, but Josh had already walked out of the barn. The man was clearly on a mission to save Mark's reputation.

Mark looked back over at his dog. "I'll see about some water and food for you."

He needed to go into the house and talk to Bailey. He wished he had some flowers to give her. Or chocolates. Women liked chocolate. He looked around the barn as though there might be something hiding in the corners he could use. There was nothing.

He walked up to the door of the house with empty hands and heard the sounds of voices coming from the kitchen. Josh was there talking. And he heard Gabe, too. Someone had opened a kitchen window and a faint trace of smoke was coming out. That's why he heard the voices.

Mark knocked on the door and, given the squeal he heard, he guessed Rosie was going to open it for him. The little girl was likely the only one happy to see him.

Rosie waited patiently while he took off his boots and then led him into the kitchen. The smoke grew stronger as he stepped inside the room.

"Oh," Bailey turned. She was fanning a burnt piece of bread. He supposed that was why her cheeks were so pink.

"Toast gone wrong?" Mark asked lightly.

"I didn't know it was inside when I turned the oven on to heat up the lasagna for dinner," Bailey said.

Mark noticed she hadn't looked at him once since he'd stepped into the room. In contrast, she couldn't seem to take her eyes off that black piece of bread.

Not that anyone else was shy about giving

him some attention, Mark noted. Gabe was staring at him like he was a specimen of some sort. Josh managed to seem both sympathetic and curious.

Little Rosie looked guilty. "I put the bread in the oven," she confessed, staring at the floor. "I wanted it warm for breakfast and I forgot."

"That's okay, sweetie," Bailey said as she reached over to hug her daughter. "Ask me if you want something heated up. But I know you're sorry. We all make mistakes sometimes."

"We sure do," Mark agreed heartily, hoping Bailey was including him in that final statement.

Bailey straightened up and eyed him directly. For a moment, Mark thought she was going to say all was well between them. But she didn't.

"When were you going to tell me?" she demanded instead and then stumbled. "Us, I mean   whcn were you going to tell us?" She gestured with her arm to include Josh and Gabe.

Mark knew she was looking at him, but he was clueless. "Tell you what?"

"About the PTSD?" she said.

Mark thought she looked a little hurt.

"I don't have PTSD," he insisted. This whole

theory had gotten out of control. "My leg got hit. That's all. My head is fine."

"It's nothing to be ashamed of," Bailey said. Now she looked offended. She clearly did not believe him.

"I don't have PTSD," Mark repeated. He wasn't sure how many times he would have to say that before anyone believed him.

"Then why did you adopt that stray dog?" Gabe asked. "I've heard of soldiers coming back and how they like to have dogs around them. Makes them feel safe. That's because of PTSD."

"Those are usually trained dogs," Mark protested. "My dog isn't the same. I don't think he can do anything. I just kind of—well, I like him."

"He fought off a pit bull," Josh said. "I'd say that's doing something."

"You like him?" Bailey asked Mark, sounding puzzled. "You don't even know him."

"I'm sure he makes you feel safe," Gabe said like that closed the argument.

"I feel good enough on my own," Mark said. "Just fine. I can take care of myself."

No one said anything at that, but Mark didn't think anyone was convinced that he was telling the truth.

"Of course you're fine," Bailey finally said

patiently as she turned to the counter and put the burnt slice of bread down on it. "Let me get this dish of lasagna in the oven and we'll eat in twenty minutes or so. Can someone get the plates out of the cabinet?"

"I'm happy to," Gabe said and walked over to the cabinet.

"I'll get glasses of water for everyone," Josh offered.

"We have iced tea, too," Bailey said as she turned to show Josh where it was.

Everyone was busy and Mark did not know what to do.

"I'll take out a pan of water to my dog," Mark decided he could use a break. Rosie wanted to go with him, but he convinced her to stay and help her mother, saying he would only take the water out and come right back.

As he started walking back to the barn, he consoled himself with the knowledge that, if he was still in the army, his troops would at least believe him when he told them something. He did not have PTSD.

Bailey put cabbage, carrots and a bit of green pepper into a small chopper so she could make some coleslaw to go with their lasagna. She wished she had lettuce, but she didn't. Cabbage kept longer on the ranch. One of the women at the funeral had made some sourdough rolls though and Bailey decided to heat them.

She felt better now that she knew what had prompted that kiss from Mark. She should have realized that a broken-down gun would bring up memories for a soldier who had been recently wounded. Although, she frowned uncertainly, she didn't think he'd been shot with a bullet. She hadn't asked, and she should have.

In any event, Josh seemed confident that PTSD was what explained Mark's actions earlier this morning. She glanced out the window and saw Mark making his way to the barn, with a pan of water in one hand and his cane in the other. He seemed a little unsteady to her, she thought suddenly. Maybe he should have a dog to trail along with him.

She should take better care of him, too. He was her best friend, even if they had been out of touch for almost ten years. She needed to help him adjust if he was having flashbacks and anything else that gave warriors nightmares.

She remembered the day he came to Dry Creek all those years ago. He'd been six years old, but he walked straight as he followed a woman social worker into the café. He'd stared ahead, his eyes cold and defiant, as the woman explained that she was looking for the Rosen ranch.

Bailey, seven years old herself, was there having an ice cream cone with her new foster parents and she knew all about social workers. She left the table and walked up to Mark and put her hand on his arm. He didn't even turn to look at her.

The social worker didn't notice her at first since she was talking to someone who was giving her directions. When she turned and saw Bailey there though the woman's face went pale.

"Move away from him," the woman ordered like Mark was a wild animal.

Bailey hadn't liked that back then. She wondered now though if Mark's PTSD wasn't partially caused by the way he was treated in the foster care system back then. At least, she felt she was on a stronger footing with him now that she knew he needed understanding. She was good at helping others.

While the lasagna was heating, Bailey went back to her bedroom and opened her suitcase. Her luggage had been near the back door of the café just like the delivery people had told her it would be. She couldn't wait to get into some real clothes. As grateful as she was to the church for the loan of the robe, it was going to the cleaners and then back to the church the first chance she got.

Within ten minutes, Bailey was back in the kitchen with her hair combed and wearing a nice pleated coral blouse. She had put a dab of lipstick on her lips and some blush on her cheeks. Not that she was trying to impress anyone, she assured herself. She just felt more confident when she looked better.

Mark came back from the barn in time to get an extra chair for the table. For months now, there had only been four people at the Sunday table—Bailey, Eli, Rosie and Gabe.

Soon everyone was settled in their chairs. She'd put a white cloth on the Formica table for dinner. The bowl of coleslaw and pan of lasagna were within everyone's reach along with the platter of warm rolls.

"Everything smells good," Mark said with appreciation in his voice. "And I like the blouse you're wearing."

The two other men looked over as though they had just noticed the change.

"Thank you," Bailey said to Mark.

Josh and Gabe both mumbled something about her looking good.

She nodded to them.

She felt the silence as they all sat there for a moment longer. This was usually Eli's time to speak. Someone needed to say a prayer and Eli wasn't here. She couldn't ask Mark; he'd made it clear where he stood on church and she didn't want to put him on the spot. And it didn't seem right to ask Josh when there was a Rosen at the table.

Finally, Bailey said, "Gabe, would you say a blessing on the meal?"

Gabe nodded solemnly as though he understood what that meant. "I miss him, too."

Gabe's prayer was short, but heartfelt.

For a time, everyone was busy eating. Bailey decided she liked having a full table for Sunday dinner. It made it feel like they were a family. By next week though, the food offerings from the funeral would be gone. She'd have to go into Miles City to buy supplies.

"Is anyone planning a trip into Miles City this week?" Bailey asked. Everyone was finishing their meal. "I'm going to need to go in."

Mark looked over and set his fork down on his plate. "Is this a doctor's appointment? For the baby?"

"No, I'm set for that," Bailey said. Eli had been generous about insurance for her and the baby. "Mrs. Hargrove has been taking me. I don't want her to have to make an extra shopping trip to the market though."

The clock on the wall struck a soft chime. It was one o'clock.

"I can take you to the doctor's now that I'm here," Mark said. "And I can take you to the grocery store, too, or I can take a list in and get what is needed. That might be better. I don't think you should be doing anything you don't have to right now."

Gabe frowned. "I can take a day off work. I think I should be the one to take you to your appointments now that Eli is gone. After all, I'm your closest adult relation."

"How do you figure?" Mark challenged the other man. "She's the widow of the son of your father's cousin. I don't think that makes you very related."

"Still," Gabe said stubbornly.

"And," Mark continued. "You don't exactly stand beside her with all this gossip."

"We can be family and disagree on things," Gabe insisted.

"Not when it comes to things like that," Mark said curtly.

Bailey felt her cheeks heat up. She wasn't used to two men quarreling over her. Although, she did admit, she was used to seeing these two particular men butt heads for other reasons. Mark, Gabe and Junior used to tussle all the time.

"There's no need for you to take off work, Gabe," Bailey said. "Although I do appreciate the offer. And, I agree. We are family—sort of, anyway."

Gabe looked smug. "I would like to talk to your doctor and ask him what sex the baby is."

Bailey was startled. "Why? He couldn't tell you anyway. I haven't had a sonogram."

"Why not?" Gabe demanded. "Surely you know that's important. Eli must have—"

"Yes," Bailey said. "Eli kept insisting and I kept saying no. I don't care if my baby is a boy or a girl. I will welcome it with joy and love either way."

"But—" Gabe started. "The will."

"I know Eli wanted a grandson," Bailey said. "Either way, I will be happy."

"We all will be," Mark said and he beamed at Bailey. "I want to know if the doctor has any recommendations though. Bed rest, that sort of thing. You must be getting close to the delivery date. I know there have to be things we should be doing. You know, vitamins. Breathing exercises. That sort of thing." Mark stopped and stared at the glass of iced tea by her plate. "Should you be drinking that? Does it have caffeine? Wouldn't milk be better?"

Bailey stared at Mark. "How many pregnant women have you known?"

"None," Mark admitted. "But I've shep- herded many a recruit through basic training. I doubt it's much different."

Bailey didn't even know what to say to that. She turned slightly and saw a smile on Josh's face.

"I have a cousin who was pregnant," Josh offered. "She would drink herbal iced tea and she was very careful so I think you're fine with that mint tea."

Bailey nodded. At least one of the men had a clue. "What should we have for dessert? There's some cherry pie and some pineapple upside-down cake."

"I like pie," Rosie offered when no one else said anything.

"I'll get it," Bailey said and put her hands on the table to make it easier to rise up.

"Let me," Mark said as he got to his feet. "You just sit there."

Bailey was happy to have the men help with the dishes, as well. She sat in one of the re- cliners in the living room with her feet up, counting her blessings. She was up to num- ber fourteen—Rosie's sunny nature—when the men announced the dishes were done and the kitchen cleared. That action had been her blessing number five.

Bailey put her hand on her stomach. The

baby had been kicking. This was her first blessing. Every time she thought of this new life, she thanked God. She knew she needed to rest up though. She'd have her hands full soon with the baby and Rosie both.

Bailey must have dozed off because the next thing she knew she saw Mark standing beside her chair. It almost seemed like a wispy dream, looking up at him while he was gazing down at her. The frown was gone from his face and she decided he had the most beautiful blue eyes she'd ever seen. And the strength in his chin was majestic. And his smile.

"Oh." She blinked and woke up completely. What was going on?

She saw Mark glance back at the kitchen door like he was checking on something. Apparently, it was all clear because he leaned down. "I wanted to check with you before—"

Bailey saw movement out of the corner of one eye.

Rosie shot through the kitchen door like a rocket and headed straight for the recliner. "Mommy, Mommy, Markie is going to—" Rosie put her hand over her mouth then and looked guilty. "I couldn't wait."

"Remember, I said I need to ask your mother first," Mark admonished the girl.

"Sorry," Rosie whispered as she looked

woefully up at Mark. He smiled down at her daughter. Bailey felt a knot in her stomach. That's what his smile looked like when she woke up.

"Rosie has agreed to take a long nap with you," Mark said and then turned to look at the girl. "Isn't that right?"

Rosie nodded, looking adorable.

"Willingly?" Bailey asked. Rosie hated naps.

The girl nodded again.

"What did you promise her?" Bailey asked Mark.

She knew her daughter. The girl had Mark wrapped around her little finger. She wondered if he knew it though.

"I told her we need to ask you first," Mark said. "Either way—"

"He's going to read me a bedtime story," Rosie interrupted, her delight shining through and her eyes dancing.

Dread shot through Bailey and she was wide awake. She remembered the question her daughter had asked last night. It couldn't be worse.

"No, sweetie, I—"

"It would just be a story out of that book of hers," Mark said, clearly confused. "A short one. It won't take but a few minutes. And you'll be there the whole time."

"Those stories are fine," Bailey said. "It's just that—well, Rosie thinks it's a daddy's job to read bedtime stories to his children."

Bailey saw the realization dawn on Mark's face. If she didn't already know that Mark did not see himself as a father kind of guy, she knew it now. His chiseled face lost its smile. His blue eyes grew distant. His back straightened as he moved back. Her heart broke a little.

"Maybe what I need to do is tell her a daytime story then," Mark offered gamely.

"What's that?" Rosie asked with a tiny frown on her forehead. "Will it make me go to sleep?"

"I think so," Mark said as he walked over to the coffee table in the living room and picked up a newspaper. "We'll pick something that happened in the daytime yesterday."

"Will it have a princess?" Rosie asked skeptically.

"I don't think so," Mark replied as he glanced at the paper. "But I think we can find out something about the little pigs that went to market."

"That one's for babies," Rosie said scornfully.

"Frogs, then," Mark said, a little desperately. "How about that?"

Rosie wasn't happy, but Bailey figured it

was better for her daughter to be a little disillusioned with Mark now than to continue to think he hung the moon. It did no one any good to believe in fantasies.

Rosie had her chin jutted out in defiance and Mark had the stoic look on his face that hid his feelings.

Bailey needed to give them both some relief. "Does anyone kiss the frog?"

A sheepish look filled Mark's face.

"A kiss is a noble thing," he finally said as he took Rosie's hand. "And frogs need to find love, too."

Bailey snorted in disbelief.

Rosie, though, nodded in acceptance. She might not be enthused like before, but she appeared willing to give Mark a chance.

"Which room do you use for naps?" Mark asked Bailey.

"The one on the left," she answered. That was Rosie's room and they often cuddled up and dozed together on the double bed there.

Bailey watched them—the tall man with his cane and the little girl who held his hand—as they went down the hall together. She wished her daughter never had to be disappointed, but the world did not consist of princesses and fairy-tale kisses. Nor did it contain many grown men who found a heart where none had been before.

Bailey stood up and started to follow them. She was never going to marry a man like Junior again and that meant she would only marry a man who could love without holding himself back. She feared that would never be Mark.

Bailey liked her daughter's room. It was painted a pale pink and the sun shone in through the white ruffled curtains on the window. A giant purple panda bear stood in one corner of the room because it did not fit in a chair. It was a treasure from the country fair last year. Eli had won it for Rosie by shooting five metal ducks in a carnival game. It had meant little to him and everything to her.

The double bed was topped by a quilt pieced together by the ladies' group at the church. Rosie had already lain down on the side of the bed nearest the folding chair they used for telling bedtime stories.

A girlish desire for love was evident all around this room, Bailey thought as Mark opened that newspaper and her daughter snuggled down into her pillow.

"It was a great day at the market," Mark began to read, his voice dramatic enough to do justice to the storytelling.

Rosie closed her eyes as Mark was in the middle of reading a list of numbers. He'd already read a bit about clouds and rain.

"There was no frog," Bailey mentioned finally, her voice drowsy. She had lain down and curled around Rosie who had already gone to sleep.

"Only found a recipe for the legs," Mark explained. "It didn't sound like it had a happy ending—at least not for the frog."

"Poor frog," Bailey murmured as she turned on her side and closed her eyes.

Mark stopped reading and silence stretched out endlessly. Bailey thought he must have left the room until she heard him walk around the bedstead.

"Just because there's no frog, doesn't mean there can't be a kiss," Mark whispered. Bailey had her eyes closed. She knew he thought she was asleep. She wasn't quite sure she'd even heard him though so she didn't respond.

More time passed. She was almost asleep when she felt the soft blanket float down over her. She definitely thought she was dreaming when she felt his lips on her forehead. Her last thought was to wonder if there was any chance Mark could fall in love with anyone. Maybe hearts could grow.

Chapter Six

Mark woke up shivering in a bitter cold bunk-house. The room was dark; the sun had not come up yet. He had slept in his jeans and socks. He could hear Josh, who had done the same, stumble around, muttering something about a tank that had run out of propane.

"Did the old man ever get the wiring out here for electricity?" Mark asked as he put the covers aside and pulled on a T-shirt. He'd forgotten that the bunkhouse stove used propane. The ranch hands had complained about it all winter long one year because the outside tank was too small and it was empty on many mornings like this.

"There's some electric around," Josh answered as he turned on a flashlight. "We can, at least, use an electric shaver over here now. And we have an electric coffeepot."

"Welcome to the twenty-first century," Mark muttered wryly. He was so chilled his teeth were chattering.

Josh chuckled. Then he shone the beam of the flashlight halfway around the large room until he settled it on a different cast-iron stove and then circled it around to the empty wood box next to it.

"That was always our backup," Mark said as he stood and wrapped a blanket around his shoulders. The bunkhouse needed more insulation in its walls and, at this time of year, the temperature frequently plunged overnight. Mark figured they'd be warmer in an army tent. "I don't suppose there's any wood piled in a shed somewhere."

"Usually, the shed is full in February," Josh said as he opened the stove door and shone his light inside. There was some newspaper laid out awaiting a match. "I doubt anyone even thought to order firewood this fall. The bunkhouse was empty."

By this time, Mark had gone to the connecting door to the foreman's suite and squinted to see inside. "I think there's some wood in the box in there. Bring the flashlight over and we'll see."

Mark and Josh each brought an armload of

chopped logs back to the wood box by their own stove.

"That'll keep us until daylight at least," Josh said as he put a few chunks into the stove. Mark had some matches and he struck one. It flared up and caught on the paper which started to curl around the wood.

"No point in either of us being up yet," Josh said as he headed toward his bunk.

"You're right about that," Mark said as he walked back to his own bed.

Once the air warmed up a little, Mark thought he would go right back to sleep, but he didn't. There was no time like a cold, dark night for a man to examine his situation and Mark couldn't help but wonder what forces in his life had led him here. He was staying in a place now where he'd long been permitted, but had never been particularly welcome. Josh was friendly, but they weren't friends. Bailey and he had played at being family to each other when they were young, but she had outgrown him and now had true family in her daughter and the coming baby.

He was like one of those trees that a man would see in the mountains in isolated parts of Montana. A traveling seed had caught in a crevice and the resulting tree grew strong, but there never would be a group of trees around it. Some would say the seed had been nothing but a mistake all along.

From the mumblings he'd heard early in life, Mark was like that seed. His father, the Irishman, had been a wandering man. His mother refused to say anything about him except that he had come whistling up from a coulee on a day close to dusk with a full pack on his back and worn boots on his feet. He'd asked for water and no one else had been home. When she asked his name, he said he was an Irishman and would say no more. He'd stayed that day and never returned. When his mother died some years later, she'd made no arrangements for Mark even though she'd known what was coming. Her family took him to a gas station by the freeway and left him there. Someone eventually called the foster care people.

Mark wasn't sure if a man was fated to be like his father, but a tree grew from the seed that it had. Nothing changed that. It was easier to be alone than to risk marrying and disappointing someone because he was totally unable to be what they wanted him to be. Maybe he could not be a family man.

Josh and Mark both slept late on Monday morning. By the time they got out of bed this time, the bunkhouse was reasonably warm.

"After breakfast, we best go see Mr. Durham

about the cattle," Mark said as he put on his Stetson and flipped up the collar on his coat. "It is rough enough weather that those cows will want to come home. We have the storm sheds in the coulee and some of them can come up to the barn."

Josh nodded. "I was thinking the same thing."

Together, they stepped out of the bunkhouse and headed for the house. It was almost eight o'clock.

"Do they still have that three-wheeler around here?" Mark asked as he carefully made his way with the cane. When he worked here, that was what they used to help move cattle in the winter.

"Eli didn't believe in getting rid of anything," Josh said. "So I'm guessing it's still in the far shed by the garage."

Mark knocked on the door to the house and Bailey answered it, wearing a green-and-white top over black slacks. She looked almost like spring.

Mark couldn't help but notice that she ignored him and smiled at Josh. She even brought a folding chair for the other man to sit on so he could take off his boots in comfort. Then she went back to the kitchen, leaving Mark leaning against the door trying to take off his boots and, he thought indignantly, he'd been wounded in the leg. Plus, he fumed as he pulled the last boot off, she had put lipstick and eye makeup on this morning and she wasn't even going anywhere. Not that he should be jealous, he told himself sternly. After all, it had been his plan to get Josh and Bailey together. He couldn't help but wonder though if she knew the other man snored. Maybe not a lot, but those things got worse as a man got older.

Mark tried not to feel left out as he stepped into the kitchen. Even Rosie didn't look up from her bowl of oatmeal. Of course, the little one looked like she was still half asleep so maybe she wasn't intentionally avoiding him.

"We're thinking of moving the cattle back this morning," Mark informed Bailey when it was clear no one was going to be chatting around the table. "Unless, that is, you need us to go into town for groceries this morning."

Mark looked at Bailey, figuring she'd have to glance at him when he talked. Instead, she focused on lifting the milk pitcher to pass it to Josh even though the other man hadn't even asked for it.

"Thanks," Josh said as he took the pitcher and poured milk into his second bowl of cereal.

Bailey just seemed to know when someone needed something, Mark thought.

"We've got plenty of groceries for today," Bailey said without even turning his way. "We should go into Miles City tomorrow morning though."

"I'll drive you," Mark announced before Josh could volunteer.

"Okay," Bailey said with as much enthusiasm as he'd expect if he had told her he was taking her to the dentist for a root canal.

Breakfast was quiet again. Mark helped himself to another slice of toast. "You make good oatmeal. Best I've had."

Bailey shrugged. "It's not hard. Just follow the directions on the box."

Mark grinned. "I found in the army that following the directions is the hard part for me."

He thought he'd make Bailey look at him and smile. She did turn her attention to him, but she frowned.

"Are you having trouble with your leg?" she asked, suddenly solicitous. "I know the doctors always give lots of orders and you don't like to follow them—you never did like doing what people said—but you have to. It's the only way to heal."

Mark opened his mouth to reassure her, but she didn't give him time to say anything.

As though it had just occurred to her, Bailey

continued. "Or, is it the other? I don't suppose they have many orders for that—"

For a second, he wasn't sure what she was talking about, but then she continued without losing a beat. "You know, the PTSD? Bad dreams, that sort of thing? Did last night go okay?"

She looked to Josh to answer that last question and the other man shrugged. "He did talk in his sleep some."

"Lots of people talk in their sleep," Mark protested firmly. "That doesn't mean it's PTSD. You could as well say it was because we were cold since the propane ran out and there wasn't enough wood to burn on a cold night."

"Oh," Bailey said, looking stricken. "We didn't order fuel for the bunkhouse. No one was there and, with Eli being the way he was, we didn't get to it."

"That's okay." Mark turned to assure her. "We'll figure something out today."

"No," Bailey said. "I'll call the propane company when they open this morning. You can't be out there with no heat and that leg of yours. It must be painful."

"I manage," Mark said. It had been stiffer than usual this morning, but he could bear it.

"You may need to call Mr. Durham, too," Josh said as he pushed his breakfast plate away and pulled his coffee cup to him. "You're as close to an owner as this ranch has at the moment and he'll want an official okay before he lets us move the cattle."

Mark was surprised. "Folks used to be a lot more trusting around here. What would he think? That we were rustling the cows?"

Josh grinned. "You'd be surprised the things that happen around here."

Mark gave that some thought. He wondered if he'd idolized the Dry Creek community in the years he'd been fighting in Afghanistan. Maybe he had, but he still thought it was the best possible place to live. He might ask Mr. Durham if he knew of any ranches for sale while they were over at his place.

Josh offered to wash the breakfast dishes and Mark went out to the shed to see if that old three-wheeler still ran. Just in case he had a hard time getting up on the thing, he didn't want an audience. These people would have him in a coffin if he fell while doing something as simple as that.

Bailey had more energy in the mornings than she had any other time of day so she sat down at the kitchen table after Mark and Josh left and made the phone calls that she needed to make. The propane tank would be filled by noon, a delivery of wood would be coming next Monday and Mr. Durham was relieved to have the Rosen cattle come home. He told her he'd help again if need be, but he was wondering if he was getting too old to be feeding cattle in the winter snows.

Rosie had sat in the recliner while Bailey talked on the telephone and the girl still seemed sleepy as Bailey brought out a coloring book, crayons and some blank paper for her daughter. She put a covering on the coffee table and got Rosie started on coloring a pirate ship. Bailey figured that would keep her daughter busy while she went through her suitcase and washed the clothes that had been to New Orleans and back.

Bailey finished her laundry and put it away before she looked at the clock and noticed it was almost noon. When she stepped over to the refrigerator to decide what to pull out for everyone to eat, she passed the window over the sink and saw that a few head of cattle were walking down the lane to the barn. She could hear more cattle bellowing and, out of habit, turned to make sure Rosie was safe. The girl was still coloring at the coffee table, but the pirate ship had joined a stack of what looked like discarded pages on the floor beside her.

"That's pretty," Bailey said softly as she

walked over and sat down in the chair close to her daughter.

Rosie smiled as she lifted up her current drawing. "I made a princess."

Bailey noticed the princess had red hair and a very bright pink dress with rows of ruffles and a matching parasol. If she interpreted everything right, there was a brown dog sitting beside the princess, too, and it looked an awful lot like that stray Mark had brought home.

"We'll have to put your picture on the refrigerator," Bailey said.

"We can't," Rosie said firmly. "I need it for Markie so he can tell me a bedtime story tonight."

Bailey held out her arms and her daughter stood up and stepped into her embrace.

"I don't think Mark will be able to tell you a story tonight," Bailey whispered against her daughter's hair. "You and me—we can make up a story though. Won't that be fun?"

Rosie didn't answer.

Bailey didn't press her point, but she noticed Rosie took her princess picture into the bedroom and set it on the chair that they used for storytelling. She wished she knew what to do for her daughter. She tried to distract her with thoughts about the new baby and that worked for a while.

For the first time in her pregnancy, Bailey hoped she would have a male child. She might be wrong, but she didn't think young boys got their hearts broken as easily as young girls. Mark had been the only young boy she'd known and she couldn't remember a time when he had been as disappointed in someone as Rosie was now. But then, she reminded herself, Mark might just have never expected anything from anyone so he had no expectations to be squashed.

They had meatloaf sandwiches for lunch and the men said they would be late for dinner since they had some work to do to get all of the cattle back home. Josh suggested she just fill and leave them two foil-covered pie tins that they could heat when they were done with the job.

Bailey was tired enough to agree. She did some housework and then put Rosie to bed early and crawled in with her. Neither one of them mentioned a bedtime story.

"Lord, bless us and keep us," Bailey whispered as she drew her daughter close and kissed her on the forehead. She couldn't help but notice the dried tears on her daughter's cheeks.

Bailey knew she needed to do better. In a few months, when the baby was here and she had her energy back, she would start looking for a husband—someone steady who would win Rosie's heart and be willing to love the both of them. She knew she had told Mark she would never get married again, but she had changed her mind.

She supposed she'd have to bring out her high heels and those clingy dresses again. She sighed. It might be longer than a few months before she was ready for that. Maybe she should try one of those internet dating sites. If they asked for requirements, she would list that the man would have to be willing to tell bedtime stories that featured princesses and fairy-tale kisses.

Chapter Seven

Mark's leg was sore the next morning so he stretched it out as he lay in his bed. These mattresses had been old and lumpy when he left years ago and they hadn't improved any. His back hurt. But the air in the bunkhouse was warm and light was streaming in the windows. They had given the place a good sweeping out yesterday and it felt like home, especially because he'd brought the dog over and the animal was now dozing on a tattered blanket in front of the propane stove.

Mark stifled a moan as he stood.

"I figured you'd regret moving all the cattle yesterday," Josh mumbled, his head still partly covered with a quilt. "I told you we could move the rest of them today."

"Today has other work that needs doing," Mark said.

Josh looked up and squinted at him. "I thought you were planning to take Bailey into Miles City today to get groceries. You left that note when we got back yesterday to remind her."

"Well, yes," Mark said as he rocked back on his bare feet a few times. That was an exercise his doctors had recommended. "That's my plan. I might buy her lunch someplace, too."

"I thought so," Josh said in triumph. "That's not work. It's a date."

"We have to eat," Mark said calmly. "Pregnant women especially need to eat regular like."

"What do you know about it?" Josh asked skeptically.

"I read about it last night," Mark said as he picked a tattered paperback off his nightstand and held it up. He'd found it on the bookshelf in the other room.

Josh started to laugh. "Don't you dare show that to Bailey."

"Why not?" Mark asked. "It's about what to do for pregnant—"

"Cows!" Josh interrupted. "It's for pregnant cows."

"Well, I know that," Mark said. "But some principles go for all species. Eating well has to be one of them."

Josh shook his head. "Just don't show her that book. That's all I have to say."

The two men finished getting dressed quickly and set out for the main house for breakfast. Bailey came to the door in her robe and instructed them to help themselves to whatever they could find to eat for the morning. She was, she said, still getting ready for the trip into Miles City.

"I hope you plan to eat breakfast before we go," Mark said as he stood by the door and took off his boots.

"I'll find something," Bailey said as though it mattered little.

Josh caught Mark's eye and cautioned him with a shake of the head.

Everyone was silent for a minute.

"I'll make you a sandwich to eat in the car," Mark finally said. "You always did like sandwiches." He tried to think of what she'd like these days. "Maybe a turkey with arugula and honey mustard?"

Bailey turned to stare at him. "I don't have arugula in the refrigerator. You probably won't even find a limp piece of lettuce. How about peanut butter and jelly?"

"That's what you liked when we were kids," Mark protested. "Your tastes—your hair—everything seems to have changed so much that I thought your taste buds would have, too."

"I might do my hair differently, but I am the same person I have always been," Bailey said emphatically.

"Peanut butter and jelly it is then," Mark said. Knowing she hadn't changed inside made him feel good.

Bailey turned to walk back to her bedroom and Mark glanced over at Josh. The other man just grinned at him.

"Wear something fun," Josh called out to Bailey. She didn't even turn and answer him.

"I hope she has sense enough to wear boots with good tread," Mark said, fretting a little now that he realized all that could go wrong with taking a pregnant female of any species out on icy streets.

When the men walked into the kitchen, they saw Rosie sitting at the table, eating a bowl of cornflakes.

"Mommy said I get to go see Mrs. Hargrove today," the girl announced a little defiantly. "She makes me cookies."

"You'll have fun," Mark said.

Rosie looked at him solemnly and then nodded. "She likes me."

Mark thought that was an unusual remark

for Rosie to make, but by then, he was reaching up into the cupboard for two more bowls.

An hour later, Mark and Bailey had dropped Rosie off with Mrs. Hargrove and they were on their way to Miles City. A paper bag of sandwiches nested on top of the cup holders between the two seats in the pickup. Bailey had eaten one sandwich, but there were two more for later if needed.

"And remember I'm going to take you to lunch," Mark said. "No fast-food place either. A regular sit-down restaurant so we can relax."

"It can't be a booth," Bailey said, a faint pink flooding her cheeks. "I can't fit in them anymore."

That book last night hadn't mentioned how beautiful a pregnant woman could be when she blushed. Mark decided Bailey looked like a Madonna painting by one of those Dutch masters. Of course, she had a lumpy knit scarf instead of one of those loose ones that wrapped around a woman's head.

"A table then," Mark said, correcting his plans with a nod. "With a white cloth on it and goblets for the water."

Bailey frowned. "It doesn't need to be that fancy. A coffee shop will do."

Mark shook his head. He couldn't imagine feeding Madonna a hamburger wrapped in a foil paper and calling it dinner. "With the baby coming, it might be a long spell before you can go out to a nice restaurant again so we should take advantage of the chance."

"But I never go to those kind of places," Bailey protested. "I don't need all that."

"I do," Mark said. He was going to insist on this.

"Oh," Bailey said, giving in sooner than he expected. "You're right," she added.

Mark congratulated himself on getting her to agree and then she kept talking.

"You've just come back to the States and you should have a special meal," she said, fussing a little with her scarf. "It would be quiet at least in a place like that."

He looked at her in confusion. "Why is that important? Are you feeling okay?"

"It's not me," she said. "In a nice place you wouldn't have to worry about any toy guns or balloons popping or anything like you might find in a fast-food place. You could relax and not worry about that PT-whatever stuff."

Mark nodded. He got the message. "I'm fine."

"You could talk to my doctor if you wanted," Bailey continued, unwinding the scarf from around her head. "He is a baby doctor, but he knows about all kinds of stress. There's no worse stress than a screaming baby." She looked at him then in dismay. "Sorry, I wasn't thinking. I meant the noise isn't as bad as war, but—well, I've heard such good things about this doctor. Several women at church went to him and recommend him highly."

Mark gave up. "Okay."

"You'll talk to him?" she asked, clearly surprised and pleased.

"Yes." He wanted to talk to her doctor and this was his chance.

A few minutes later, Mark added, "What kind of food do you want? I don't know what kinds of restaurants we can find in Miles City, but I'm sure they have a nice steak place."

All Montana towns of any size had a good steak place, Mark figured.

"I've heard there's one that has grilled mushrooms that are very good," Bailey offered. "Over on Hamilton Street. It has fish and steak. Junior always promised to take me there. We never made it though."

Mark wanted to ask her why she had married Junior in the first place, but he didn't want to spoil the day.

"Anything else you want to do while we're in Miles City?" he asked.

"We could see if we could find one of those

whirly-twirly things or a Ferris wheel," she said, her tone serious.

"But we can't," Mark sputtered, turning to look at her in astonishment. That book he'd read on cows never said anything about this kind of thing. "You're pregnant!"

"I know," Bailey said with a sigh. "It's just that there's so much I can't do—I can't even get into my regular clothes. Or climb stairs. Or sleep through the night without needing to get up to go to the bathroom a million times. I just wish we could have a little fun like we used to when we were kids."

"I don't remember that much fun," Mark said cautiously.

"Just being with you was fun for me," she said.

"You were the one who made things special," he replied. And it was true. Bailey had been his world.

They were silent for a while and then Bailey said, "I guess I'm just anxious for the baby to come. I'm tired of waiting."

"I can understand that," Mark said. "Maybe the doctor's office will be fun."

Bailey looked at him skeptically. "He doesn't even have suckers to give out. Or balloons."

"Well, after we see your doctor, I thought we'd go to the place where Arnold works,"

Mark said, knowing it was lame, but it was the best he could do. "Josh said they have some good shirts with long sleeves. Department store sizes don't always fit me right. Maybe they'll have some western jewelry, too. Or leather purses."

"That will be nice," Bailey said, looking pleased. "I used to go there with Eli to buy his shirts. Arnold was always glad to see us when we went, too. I think he misses the ranch."

Mark nodded. "Well, then."

He decided to quit while he was ahead. Maybe he'd ask the doctor if there was an exciting restaurant in Miles City, maybe one of those that had a big fish tank inside or travel pictures on the walls. That might make Bailey feel like she'd had an adventure.

Bailey had to walk slowly as they headed to the doctor's office and Mark insisted on her holding his arm, but she was nervous every step of the way. She probably wouldn't even be able to walk up to a Ferris wheel let alone take a ride on one.

"Quite a few doctors share this reception area," she said as Mark stood on a rubber mat and scraped the snow off his boots. "Five or six, at least."

She hadn't really thought about Mark being

inside the waiting room with all these pregnant women. It was rare for a man to be part of these midday appointments. She wasn't quite sure how to warn Mark though.

"There will be other patients," she said. "Pregnant ones. Lots of them."

He only nodded.

"My doctor might not even be available," Bailey added. He always said he could squeeze her in if she wanted to see him about something, but it might be a busy day and he might not have time to see Mark, as well.

Mark opened the door and they both hurried into the warmth of the shared waiting room. A dozen or so women looked up to see who they were.

Bailey nodded. She knew most of them even though they all had different doctors. She blushed when she saw the women each looking Mark over and giving her a subtle nod of approval.

"I'll talk to the receptionist," Bailey said as she let go of Mark's arm.

She didn't want to give anyone the wrong impression. She turned to the women sitting around in matching chairs. "Mark is helping me because of the icy sidewalks."

The women nodded and Bailey watched as Mark went and sat right in the middle of the women. She held her breath, sure he would be shy with so many women. To her surprise, he didn't seem to mind at all. She frowned a little. He never used to be that comfortable with girls when they were growing up together. She was the only one he would even talk to. She wasn't sure how she felt about that—seeing him chatting away like the women were his buddies.

Her doctor insisted on seeing Bailey first and said he'd save another ten-minute slot for Mark.

"You need to rest more," the doctor said as he helped Bailey to her feet after their discussion. "You're going to need your strength."

The nurse called Mark's name as Bailey came back into the waiting room.

The women barely let her sit down before they leaned over toward her.

"Well," one of them said with a dramatic sigh. "That certainly isn't Mrs. Hargrove with you today."

"No, I—" Bailey started to explain and stopped.

"Is he the one?" another woman asked, making a big point of fanning herself with one of the clinic flyers. "If he is, he's hot, hot, hot."

The woman grinned as she put down the flyer.

"The one what?" Bailey asked, confused.

She had been in several pregnancy preparation groups with these women, but they hadn't talked about that many personal things.

"You know, the one who had Junior so bothered," a different woman said with a smile. "Remember, you told us he'd given you a hard time about a man. I would guess Mark would give any man a run for his money."

Bailey had forgotten about that one time she had talked about Junior.

"Oh, no," Bailey said. "There was no man when Junior was saying those things. Mark has been my friend since we started the first grade. He's been gone for ten years and hasn't even been back in the country for more than a week or so."

"Oh," they said, almost in unison. Then they followed it with a collective disappointed sigh.

"You're sure you're just friends?" the first woman asked. "He seems like a very fine man."

"And so nice," another woman offered. "He was so interested in us."

"He wanted to know all about what a pregnant woman needed to eat," another one of them said. "We gave him some pointers on vitamins."

"He made me sandwiches for the trip in this morning," Bailey offered what she could and the women smiled as though that's what they would have expected.

"We can get hungry all of a sudden," one of the women noted. "He's got a good head on his shoulders."

"We're just friends though," Bailey added to be sure they knew.

The women nodded, but she could tell they didn't have their hearts in it. Bailey decided that all pregnant women must like a good romance story. She wished she had one to tell them.

It wasn't until she and Mark were slowly walking back to the pickup that Bailey realized that, even if her relationship with Mark wasn't what the women thought, she had been proud of him. With Junior, she had introduced him and hoped for the best. No one seemed to applaud him. She realized later that he had a reputation for playing fast and loose with women. No one had told her about that, but she figured that was the reason he'd gone all the way to Los Angeles to convince her to marry him. Eli wanted him to find a wife and all of the women around Dry Creek were wise to him.

She and Mark got settled into the cab of the pickup and Bailey asked, "Did the doctor help you?"

"He sure did," Mark said as he pulled a

white paper bag out of his pocket. "He gave me some sample pills."

"For panic attacks?" Bailey asked in surprise. She didn't think they gave those pills out like that.

Mark shook his head as he started the engine. "They're vitamins. The ladies in the waiting room recommended them. Even if you haven't been taking them until now, they'll still help."

Bailey looked at him in exasperation. "You talked to the doctor about me the whole time, didn't you? You were supposed to talk about yourself."

"I'm fine," Mark said as he pulled out into the street. "You're the one having a baby. And—" he glanced over sternly "—the women said you need to be resting more. From now on, Josh or I will do the cooking."

Bailey waved the concern away. "I'm not doing hard cooking. Mostly it's just warming up things. And I get plenty of rest. The doctor is always saying I need more rest. But I can't live my life asleep."

Since it was not even eleven o'clock, they decided to go see Arnold about the shirts Mark wanted.

At first, Bailey wasn't going to go into the shop with Mark, but it was cold outside and she did want to say hello to Arnold. She'd felt bad when the older man left his job just because he was worried about all of that gossip about her and a mystery man.

Mark insisted on holding her arm as they made their way down the sidewalk to the door and Bailey was grateful for the support. She'd heard other women complain about feeling like hippos in the last weeks of their pregnancy and she knew what they meant when she started to feel her feet slip on the ice. She probably would have fallen without Mark's help.

The store was warm and a bell tinkled when they stepped inside. No one was visible at first, but then Bailey saw Arnold coming out from a back room wearing a tailor's apron over his clothes. Shelves of men's slacks lined one side of the shop and hats of all kinds hung on the opposite wall. The rest of the store was filled with racks of suits and shirts of all colors— bright red, black-and-gray plaid, yellow, beige and blue. She loved the brightness.

"Bailey!" Arnold called out, clearly glad to see her.

Then the older man ignored Mark and even Bailey as he hurried over to pull the blinds on the front store window. Following that, he reached under the covering and flipped the small Open sign to Closed.

"What's happening?" Bailey asked as she took a step closer to Mark.

Mark looked puzzled, too, as he studied the older man.

"I thought Eli would be enough, but now he's gone," Arnold muttered, almost to himself. His short gray hair stood out in tufts on the side of his balding head. He looked distraught, but determined.

He turned so he had his back to Mark and was facing Bailey.

"Is something wrong?" Bailey asked.

"No, nothing's wrong. I'm just working up my nerve to have a private conversation and I don't want the whole town of Miles City to hear what I have to say."

Bailey was worried. Was he going to yell about something? "Did Eli—I mean, did the ranch not give you the right amount of pay when you left?"

That was the only thing she could imagine that would put that pained look on Arnold's face and have anything to do with Eli. She hoped the amount owed wasn't too high.

"I don't imagine you want your job back." Bailey kept talking. She did that when she was nervous. "It's the cold time of year. Your rheumatism would act up something fierce. But if you really want it back, we could—"

"I've decided it's time to do my duty," Arnold interrupted, the effort of talking clear on his face. "Just give me a minute."

Arnold walked behind a counter and pulled out a wooden chair that he shoved over to where Bailey stood. Then he used the chair for balance as he slowly knelt down in front of her. She winced along with Arnold as his knees hit the hard floor.

Everyone waited as Arnold caught his breath.

Bailey wondered if he would mind if she sat in that chair now that it was so convenient and he was no longer using it. She was feeling a little faint. Maybe it was too warm in here.

Arnold's face shone with perspiration, but he seemed intent as he extracted a white handkerchief from a pocket and wiped his forehead.

"Are you all right?" Mark asked as he stepped closer to the older man. Bailey shared the same concern.

Arnold turned to frown at Mark. "I wouldn't need to do this if you were doing the right thing. When I saw you here, I thought it was why you came back. But Josh tells me it's not."

Mark looked at Bailey as though she might know what was going on. She shook her head; she didn't have a clue.

Arnold turned back to her and cleared his

throat. Then he began to speak formally, "Miss Bailey, I would like to honor me—mean, I would like the honor of having your hand in marriage."

"What?" Bailey exclaimed, her voice faint.

"I'm willing to marry you," Arnold said, his voice regaining its strength. "Right and proper. That baby of yours needs a father and I'm willing. If Eli were still here, it would be different, but he's not. I am though and I stand ready."

"I don't think—" Mark began and Arnold looked at him sternly.

"No, you probably don't think," Arnold said, scolding Mark. "I don't know why men aren't willing to shoulder their duty these days. You should be the one marrying Bailey."

"But Mark isn't the father," Bailey said, her voice rising defiantly. "And you know that very well, Arnold Green."

"Well, I'm not the father either," Arnold retorted emphatically. "But Junior's dead. There's nothing we can do to bring him back. So, we need someone to step up and do the job."

Bailey wondered if any woman anywhere had received a less flattering proposal.

"No one needs to marry me," she said, feeling a headache coming on. "I'm a grown woman and I can take care of myself and my children. Single parents do it all the time."

She decided she better sit down on that chair after all. She was already a little woozy. Mark was right there steadying her or she might have tipped sideways before she made it to the chair.

"See," Arnold said gruffly. "You need help."

"Well, maybe I do." She had to admit that. "But just until the baby comes."

"Any pregnant woman or animal needs some assistance," Mark said, agreeing with her forcefully. "It says so in the book."

"What book?" Bailey asked, feeling a little disoriented.

"You read a book about pregnancy?" Arnold asked in astonishment, looking at Mark with some respect. "Maybe you will do as a husband after all."

"I prefer to arrange my own life," Mark said. "I'm sure Bailey does, too."

"Well," Arnold said as he pulled himself to his feet holding on to the back of the chair Bailey was using. Once upright, he brushed his slacks with his hands and then adjusted his apron. "You have my offer, but I'll put it on hold until you both come to your senses. I will expect you to inform me when you two have the situation in hand."

Bailey was going to respond, but she

couldn't think of anything to say. She wondered if she was experiencing some low blood sugar. Maybe she should have eaten two of those sandwiches that Mark had brought along for her.

"Now," Arnold said just like they hadn't had their discussion. "What can I help you with today?"

The shock of that change of topic stopped everyone.

"I need some shirts," Mark finally said. "A few work shirts. A white shirt. And a nice black suit that works for funerals and such."

"I suppose you were wishing you had one at Eli's send-off," Arnold said in a friendly clerk voice. "You can always rent one, you know."

Mark nodded. "I have long arms so I'm hard to fit. It's best that I have my own. And I don't want to be caught up short again."

Arnold turned, walked to the counter and came back with a measuring tape.

Mark stood patiently while Arnold measured him.

Bailey smiled quietly. Now that the drama was over, she realized what a pleasure it was to watch Mark.

Twenty minutes later, he was at the counter paying for a pile of clothes and two top hats.

Mark had bought the small top hat as a gift for her daughter.

"Rosie will be excited," Bailey said quietly. "I can't believe they had such a small top hat. I thought we'd have to make one out of black construction paper."

Mark shook his head. "That wouldn't stay on her head. Not when she's tapping her heart out. And she'll want to take it off for when she makes her bow at the end. I thought we'd have to buy one online though from a party store."

Arnold finished bagging the shirts and put a cleaner's plastic cover around the suit.

"Too bad they don't have canes here," Mark said as he paid for his new clothes. "Short ones."

"They have canes at the drug store on the next street north of here," Arnold said. "I don't know the sizes, but some of them adjust quite a bit."

"I have a cane for her," Bailey said. "Mrs. Hargrove had one that she used for Sunday school programs over the years. It's kid size. And we bought several taps for her shoes already. And she has a dress to wear that works. She's already rehearsed some."

"That's good then," Mark said as he picked up the two bags that held his new clothes.

Mark turned around and then looked at her.

"I'm going to have to make a couple of trips," he said. "My cane takes one arm and I only have two."

"That's okay," Bailey said as she stood. "I can get myself out to the pickup."

"Not on my watch," he said as he walked over to where she sat and set the bags on the floor. "I'll take you in the first trip."

By the time Mark settled her in the pickup and returned to get his bags, Bailey saw the first snowflake fall.

"Maybe we should take a rain check on that fancy dinner," she said when he climbed back into the cab. She had counted a dozen more flakes that had fallen in the time he'd been gone. "We'll do best to get the groceries and head on home."

"I don't want you out in a blizzard, that's for sure," Mark said as he put on his seat belt and turned the key in the ignition. "Did you make a list? I can go in and get what we need."

Bailey nodded. "The only thing I don't have on the list is dog food. I didn't know if you wanted to get it at the grocery store or the farmer's co-op—it's cheaper there."

"I figure the grocery store given the snow," Mark said.

Bailey gave him directions to the store she usually used and a half hour later they were loaded up and leaving the parking lot to head for the freeway.

"I can drive through some place and get hamburgers for us," Mark said as they pulled onto a street with several fast-food restaurants. "You pick which one."

Mark pulled up to the one she chose and they ordered from the window.

Minutes later, Bailey accepted the foil-wrapped burger he handed her and opened it, breathing in the blissful aroma of warm bread and grilled meat.

Mark chuckled. "You still look like a Madonna."

"Huh?" she turned to him.

"It's nothing," Mark said. "I think I'm beginning to see that you really haven't changed much since grade school. Not in the important ways."

Bailey thought about it. "I never did need fancy things to make me happy even though I do think we should go out to a nice dinner sometime."

"When there's not a storm coming," Mark said.

"I'm going to hold you to that," Bailey said and took a bite out of her hamburger.

A few minutes later she put her food down. After one bite she started to fret. "I want you to know that Arnold is wrong. There's no reason you should feel beholden to marry me. I'll be fine."

"I know you will," Mark said. "But I can't hold it against Arnold that he cares about you and the baby and Rosie. I've been worried about all of you myself."

"You don't think he'll go find someone else and suggest they marry me, do you?" Bailey asked. She knew she should leave this alone, but she couldn't.

"No, I don't," Mark replied confidently. "I've already thought about all of the single men around."

She gasped. "You'd set me up with somebody?"

"No," Mark said patiently. "I just told you. I couldn't think of anyone good enough."

Bailey didn't know what to say to that.

"Well, don't set me up," she finally managed to say.

Bailey waited to see if he had anything to add, but he apparently didn't. She told herself she never should have asked her question. She did note that he didn't seem to have any remote notion about marrying her himself. That alone made his position clear.

Mark drove carefully all of the way home. He might never want to get married, Bailey thought, but she knew he would take care of her. She couldn't really ask anything more of a friend. Except perhaps—

"That white shirt," she said when they were about halfway home. "Do you plan to go to church this coming Sunday?"

Mark was silent for longer than she had hoped.

"I might go," Mark finally said. "I don't want people to think I've been run off with their comments about my dog."

Bailey nodded. There was a chance Mark would learn to care about others, maybe even to love them. He was trying. She'd leave the rest to God.

Chapter Eight

Mark woke up early on Sunday and wished he could stay in bed. But he had to go to church this morning. He heard a whining and rolled over to find his dog standing beside the door. Mark vowed to build a doggie door in the bunkhouse as soon as he could. He didn't know why it hadn't been done already.

"Just a minute," Mark muttered as he stood up and wrapped the blankets around him. Then he fumbled around until he could put his feet into the pair of slippers he'd found in the closet off the laundry room. With that, he walked over to the door and let the dog out into the dim light of morning.

Mark noted more snow had fallen during the night. He knew folks in this kind of country didn't let a few feet of snow stop them from going to church, but he wished they did.

When they had arrived back to the ranch yesterday, he'd had mail. Mrs. Hargrove had sent him an embossed card, asking him to come and talk to her kindergarten Sunday school class about what it was like to be in the military. She said he could pick the date, but she hoped he would do the talk on the eighth, which was today, since next Sunday would be Valentine's Day weekend and she planned to do a whole section on love.

Mark wasn't sure about her doing war one week and love the next, but he knew the older woman would find a way to make it fascinating to the children.

When his dog came back inside, Mark sat down on the bench by the door and used a ragged towel to dry the mutt off. By the blissful look in the animal's eyes, he seemed to enjoy the snow, although he never did want to stay outside for long. Come to think of it, maybe the canine liked the drying-off time and not the snow itself.

"We need to get you a name, don't we, partner?" Mark murmured once the dog was dry. He noticed the animal was already looking better than it had when he first saw it. It no longer looked like a stray.

Thinking of looks, Mark wondered if he should wear his army uniform for the class today and decided he would. He had a few shiny medals and bits of color here and there that would give the children something to look at if they didn't want to listen. Of course, he'd have to say something.

As he sat there wondering what to say to the children, more light streamed into the bunkhouse and finally it was time to get up.

Mark and Josh were seated at the breakfast table with Bailey and Rosie when Mark gave up on trying to figure out what to say to the class.

"Are there any Bible verses about how to do in your enemies?" Mark asked as he buttered a second slice of toast. "To really get them good?"

That woke everyone up. Even Rosie looked alarmed.

"The Bible says we should do good to our enemies," Bailey said firmly. She wore her faded robe over a blouse and had a bit of jam on her chin. Her hair was tied up in a blue bandana. "We don't do them in. We need to turn the other cheek. Humble, like. That sort of thing."

"I can't tell the boys and girls to turn the other cheek," Mark protested. "They need to grow up in the real world."

Rosie grinned. Her hair needed to be combed

and she had a crooked bow pinned in it, but he knew she was going to say her piece. "All the boys in Mrs. Hargrove's class don't treat their enemies very nice. I know that. You better not go near those Baker boys."

"Do they bother you?" Mark asked, frowning. He didn't like the thought of anyone pestering his Rosie.

"Not anymore they don't," Rosie said with extreme satisfaction as she took another spoon of her flakes.

Bailey looked curious, too, by now. She'd wiped off the jam while her daughter was talking. Then she slipped her robe off like she was going to leave the table. Mark thought she looked particularly fetching in the black silk top she had been wearing under the robe. It had crystal buttons and pleats all the way around the front. No wonder she wanted a robe over it while she ate jam and toast.

Bailey started to rise, but she was still studying her daughter. "What did you do to those boys?"

"I popped them on their heads with Mrs. Hargrove's cane," the girl said in a very matter-of-fact manner. "I didn't break their heads, but they felt it. And I could reach them because her cane is longer than their arms. They couldn't get me back."

"Well, I don't think that's—" Bailey said, her face troubled.

"She must have had to," Mark said to stop the scold he could see was coming. "You see, that's the problem with enemies. They don't always want to be nice to us just because we're being nice to them."

"That's when we pray," Bailey countered as she picked up her robe from the chair and folded it over her arm.

Mark smiled. "You used to hit boys on the head with an old broom when they were teasing me. Remember, when I first moved here. I think I was still six-years-old and finding my way around."

"I was saving their lives," Bailey said self-righteously as she looked him in the eye unflinchingly. "It was an act of mercy. I knew if you got your hands on them that it would be much worse for them even though they were bigger than you."

"So it was a preemptive strike," Mark nodded. "The military knows that strategy, too."

"You can't tell those children it's ever okay to attack their enemies," Bailey said firmly. "We'd be at war all over the place if we did that."

"That pretty well sums up where we are," Mark agreed. "Just check your world news."

Everyone at the table looked at him and he wondered if he should simply refuse to talk to the kindergarten class.

"Maybe I should stay home," Mark said. That sounded good to him.

Josh grunted. "Maybe you should all go. It sounds like you have a good discussion right there with everyone. The peace people. The war people. You have it all."

Mark liked the thought of them all going up front together. "How about it?"

"I'll go," Rosie said, eagerly.

"You're already in that class, sweetie," Bailey said. "We'll have to talk to Mrs. Hargrove and see if it's okay if you are also part of Mark's lesson."

"You're coming, too, aren't you?" Mark asked Bailey.

She nodded. "I feel I need to get to know the Baker boys better." She turned to Rosie. "Maybe we should make them some cookies tomorrow."

Rosie looked horrified. "I don't think so."

"Well," Bailey said. "We'll talk about it later. We best get going or we'll be late."

Mark wore his uniform and Bailey wore enough black to be in the military, too. She managed to look the part, too, because she stood straight and looked all of the kindergarten students in the eye.

"We have with us Army Sergeant Mark Dakota from Afghanistan and his friend, Bailey Rosen," Mrs. Hargrove introduced them. She had suggested Rosie sit with her class until they did a segment on how to handle bullying. She also cautioned all three of them not to name the Baker boys.

"We don't need to name them," Rosie had whispered to Mark. "Everybody will know who you're talking about anyway—especially the other boys."

Mark nodded. Children did usually know those kinds of things.

"The sergeant is going to tell us about war and what it's like to face a real enemy," Mrs. Hargrove said.

The half hour went quickly. The boys wanted to know if he got to carry a gun and the girls wanted to know if he got to keep all his medals or if he had to turn them in like library books when he gave back his uniform. He explained that every one of them, including the uniform, were his.

Then the Baker boys wanted to know what to do about an enemy who was bigger than them. Mark talked to the boys a little and found out that their uncle, who was living with them and their mother, was hitting them. Mark could see they were scared of the man and he offered to go talk to their uncle. The boys huddled together looking at him, clearly torn between hope of what could change and terror of what could go wrong.

"I think it's for the best, boys," Mrs. Hargrove finally said, encouraging them. "I'll go with Mr. Dakota to be sure your uncle gets a proper invite to church."

Mark hadn't planned on suggesting the man come to church, but he did think it was good for Mrs. Hargrove to go with him when he met with the uncle.

Bailey suggested a couple of verses for the children to learn and they seemed satisfied with the lesson. Mrs. Hargrove said a prayer before she dismissed the class. When it was over, most of the children came up to reverently touch the medals Mark had on his chest. He had a Purple Heart and a couple of other golden medals.

When the children left, Mrs. Hargrove asked Mark to stay back for a few minutes. Bailey took Rosie upstairs.

The older woman gestured for Mark to sit and he did, even though the chairs were too small for him and he sort of teetered on the edge of one.

"I want to thank you for offering to take up for the Baker boys," she said.

Mark shrugged. "It's nothing."

The older woman gave a sad smile. "It reminds me of how we failed you when you were a boy here."

"No one failed me," Mark said.

"I know that's how you feel," Mrs. Hargrove said. "But those Baker boys remind me of you. We never taught you to trust people to help you. We could have probably gotten Eli to be more welcoming to you. He treated you like a hired hand and you were just a boy. We never even taught you to trust God."

"That's okay," Mark rushed to assure her. "I do all right."

"Do you?" she asked. "Or is it only that you have accepted too little in life and have yet to face a problem so big that you can't take care of it by yourself?"

Mark didn't want to answer, but Mrs. Hargrove kept looking at him with worry in her eyes.

"I don't want to be a hypocrite," Mark finally said. "I'm not going to expect God to get me out of trouble when I haven't bothered with Him before. That doesn't seem right."

"It would be all right with Him," Mrs. Hargrove said confidently. "God doesn't care when you turn to Him—just that you do. He'll take you any time. And no one deserves it so don't let that stop you."

Then she reached over to a nearby table and picked up a small booklet that she held out to him. "I give this to all my students so I'm sure I gave you a copy years ago when you were in my class."

"I do remember the blue on the cover," Mark muttered. He felt awkward taking the pamphlet, but he didn't know what else to do. By then, they could hear the music starting upstairs in the sanctuary and Mark decided that was his cue to leave.

"Thank you," he said and put the pamphlet in his pocket.

Mrs. Hargrove sat there silently.

"I'll see you upstairs," he said as he started to walk out of the room. When he got to the door, he turned around and spoke softly. "I want to thank you for caring about me, Mrs. Hargrove. I might not know how to trust, but I do appreciate you caring for me all those years ago and now, too."

"Well, then," the older woman said as she stood with a smile on her face that looked genuine and warm. "We have hope for you yet, Mark Dakota. I have faith you'll come to our Lord in His time. Let's go up to church."

Bailey had saved a place for him and he felt good slipping into the pew beside her and Rosie. He let the words of the sermon flow over him. He couldn't remember now why he had decided he'd had enough of church when he was twelve years old. If he didn't know better, he would have thought that Mrs. Hargrove had instructed the pastor to preach on how much God loves people and how they're to love each other.

He figured the man's sermon even did some good. When he walked out of the sanctuary after the service was over, several of the ranchers who had given him such a hard time the week before crowded in to shake his hand. Half of them even asked how his dog was doing and said they were glad he'd taken the poor mutt home with him.

He was thinking how well it was all working out when one of the ranchers cleared his throat and spoke.

"We hope that dog gives you comfort," he said, his gravelly voice thick with emotion. "None of us would have objected if we'd known about your troubles. I have a nephew who suffers from the same thing. He's going to beat it though. He's got him a doctor and everything."

Mark stared at the man in confusion.

"Josh told us," another one said.

Mark swallowed and forced the tension back from his voice. "Josh is mistaken. I don't have PTSD."

Some of the men looked at him in alarm.

"Is that a symptom?" one of them asked. "Forgetting, like?"

"No," Mark answered sharply. "I don't forget anything."

The whole circle of men shifted on their feet, but they were silent.

"Any of you men know the Baker boys?" Mark finally asked when the conversation seemed stopped.

They all nodded, looking relieved to have a change of conversation.

"The man they call uncle," Mark continued. "Is he a real one?"

They no longer looked so comfortable.

"I hate to say bad about anyone," one rancher finally mumbled.

That was news to Mark. They had seemed ready enough to do that when they were against him and his dog.

"Their mother claims the man is," someone finally admitted. "I knew her family though and she didn't have a brother. No sister either. As to that husband of hers who left, I don't figure any of his worthless family would be showing up. They're all out east someplace and he never mentioned any closeness to any of them."

"What's this uncle do for work?" Mark asked.

A few of the men snorted in disgust.

"Nothing more than he can help," a man finally answered. "I think the family gets by on some kind of government assistance. And the church gives them food baskets here and there."

"Thanks," Mark said and then the conversation died down again.

"If you go out there," a man in suspenders said then. "I'll go with you if you want. I wouldn't recommend you go out there alone."

"Thanks, but Mrs. Hargrove offered to go with me," Mark said.

The men nodded in seeming approval.

"She still got that cane of hers?" one of them asked. "It might be good for her to take it along."

Mark smiled. "I wouldn't want her cane to get scuffed up." He looked down. "Of course, I always have my cane with me. It's sturdy enough to be knocked around some."

The men seemed satisfied with that and they turned to leave with their respective wives.

Mark saw Bailey and Rosie waiting for him.

It was a small thing, but it made him feel good to have someone. He reached into his pocket and felt the pamphlet that Mrs. Hargrove had given him. He did remember it from her class. He'd thrown it away back then and never read it. But maybe he'd look it over this afternoon after dinner. He owed the older woman the courtesy of doing that.

Bailey was glad when one of the women from the church gave her a frozen casserole during the coffee time, explaining that she knew the food from the funeral was probably gone by now and she knew how hard it was to cook during the last month of a pregnancy.

It was snowing in earnest by the time they started home from church. Bailey had her coat wrapped tight around her and she had bundled up Rosie, too. The pickup's heater was pushing out hot air and the little girl was leaning against her side.

"When are you planning to go see the Bakers?" Bailey asked as she shifted so she could put her arm around Rosie.

Mark looked over. "Mrs. Hargrove and I thought we'd go late tomorrow morning, around ten thirty. She's going to call and see if they would be available then."

"Just like a proper appointment," Bailey said in approval.

"They won't want you to come," Rosie muttered softly.

Bailey looked down at her daughter. "That's a good reason for us to make them some cookies. Everyone likes company when they bring cookies."

Rosie looked up, eyeing her skeptically. "What kind of cookies?"

"How about oatmeal raisin?" Bailey asked. She knew that was Rosie's favorite cookie so she figured they were popular with others her age.

"Let's leave out the raisins," Rosie said grimly. "We don't want to run out in case I need some raisins in my cookies."

Bailey was aghast. "We're making the cookies to share with the Baker boys. We want them to be the best cookies we can make. Maybe they'll want to be our friends, but even if they don't, it's a gift so it has to be nice."

Rosie grunted, but she didn't say anything more. She snuggled down next to her mother's arm until her little nose was burrowed in the folds of Bailey's coat. Bailey wondered if her daughter was getting enough sleep. She was usually full of light and sunshine, but lately she'd been subdued.

"Thanks," Bailey said as Mark gently swerved the pickup to avoid a rut in the road. He was being careful to give them a smooth ride and it wasn't easy due to the falling snow. The view through the windows was mostly white. The windshield wipers were pushing the falling snow off the glass and the heater was melting some of the accumulated flakes, but it was clear a blizzard was underway.

"I'll be glad when we're home and out of this weather," Mark said and it made her feel good.

"I'll be glad when we're home, too," she said.

She could see the tracks of Josh's pickup since he'd gone ahead of them after church. His tracks would lead on past the Rosen Ranch though, as Josh was planning to visit his uncle's family this afternoon.

Because of the weather forecast, Gabe had called last night to say he was staying in Miles City this weekend. He sounded sorry about it and she realized how much a part of his life these Dry Creek visits were. He had a long-standing agreement with Mrs. Hargrove to rent her room and bath over her garage for every Saturday night. Bailey knew the black dress the older woman had worn to Eli's funeral had been one of those extras that she had deemed affordable because of Gabe's rental income.

Bailey was relieved when Mark turned the

pickup into the lane leading up to the house. It hardly seemed possible, but the storm looked like it was getting worse.

Mark drove the vehicle up close to the front door. By that time, Rosie was sleeping.

"I'll come around and carry Sleeping Beauty into the house," Mark said with a fond glance at Rosie.

"That would be nice," Bailey said.

"But," Mark said and gave her a stern look. "You have to promise to wait right here until I get back. I don't want you to try to walk into the house by yourself. There's likely a layer of ice under this snow and you'll go flying like a Frisbee."

"I will," Bailey said softly. It wasn't a hardship to promise anything to a man like this who cared about her, even if his caring wasn't of a passionate, husbandly kind.

She waited for Mark to come around to her door.

"Time to wake up, sweetie," Bailey whispered to her daughter when she saw the outline of Mark against her window. The girl burrowed in deeper.

Mark opened the door and cold air blew inside. Rosie groaned and opened her eyes.

"I'll need you to hang on again," Mark said

to the girl. "I have my cane so I can only use one arm."

Rosie woke up more than Bailey expected and smiled. "Horsie?"

"Yeah," Mark said and gave a guilty glance at Bailey. "It's necessary."

Bailey nodded. Her daughter was delighted and scrambled over Bailey.

Mark slid his coat down and Rosie wrapped herself around his back. Bailey reached over and adjusted the coat so it covered them both.

"Hold tight now," Mark said.

"I know," Rosie assured him.

Mark stepped away from the pickup and walked the few steps to the front door. They'd left the door to the house unlocked and he opened it easily and walked inside. Bailey knew it would be warm because they had left the furnace on low.

Before she had time to get chilled, Mark was back for Bailey. He helped her slide out of the cab and offered her his arm. She held the covered dish on one side and used her other hand to hold on to Mark's arm. Together they slowly walked to the door and he opened it.

Mark saw that she was settled before he left to drive the pickup over to its regular parking place. Bailey walked into the kitchen, set the covered dish on the counter and put some hot water on to boil. She figured tea or hot chocolate would warm everybody up while they waited for their dinner to cook.

Then she peeled back the foil on the covered dish and nodded to herself. It looked good with lots of spicy taco meat, chips and chopped onion. Everything was covered with a thick sprinkling of grated cheddar cheese. She decided to let it all thaw a little more while the oven heated.

"What's to eat?" Rosie asked from the doorway to the kitchen. The girl had taken her coat off and was holding her arms close to her chest to keep warm. "I'm hungry."

"Taco casserole," Bailey said. "When the oven starts to heat up, it will take the chill out of the air."

Rosie nodded. "I like taco stuff."

"Me, too," Bailey said. "And I'm going to cook some corn to go with it."

Mark was back in the living room when she returned. The casserole was in the oven and the corn was waiting on the stove for the last-minute heating.

Bailey sat down in the recliner and tried to get herself comfortable. No one had ever told her before how many aches and pains a pregnant woman could have. Her ankles were swollen, her joints ached and her spine acted like it was burdened with one of those prize-winning pumpkins strapped to her back. Even her eyeballs hurt.

Mark had his damp coat draped over a side chair and his boots sitting on the welcome rug. The scent of wet wool was starting to mix with the smell of the casserole. Somehow that wet wool odor seemed very male to her, reminding her that it was nice to have a man in the house for Sunday dinner.

"I brought some laundry over this morning when I came to breakfast," Mark said. "After we eat, I'll do a couple of loads. Some sheets and towels."

"I could do it for you," Bailey said with a yawn, caught in the pleasantness of Mark's company. Then she remembered she was moving slow and would be doing good to get through the upcoming meal. As she grew warmer, her eyes started to droop. She forced herself to open them wide. That's when she saw Mark watching her with a smile on his face.

"You just sit tight and take a nap if you can," Mark said. "It's just Rosie and me here. I'll read some until dinner is ready and we'll find something for her to do."

"You'll wake me?" she asked.

"Of course."

Bailey smiled as she curled up in the chair. Mark might not be interested in getting married, but he sure sounded domesticated. "Don't let me forget the oven either. In thirty minutes or so, it will be ready. I set the timer, but it doesn't always work."

"Don't worry," Mark said. "I've got it all covered."

Bailey's mind drifted easily then. The howl of the wind was soothing. The spicy smell from the kitchen was comforting. And she was so very tired. It felt good to have her family safe inside when the storm was swirling outside. It never even occurred to her to question the picture in her mind when she thought of family. It was Rosie and her with Mark right between them as though he were their anchor. He sure was a nice man.

Chapter Nine

Mark read until he finished every line of the cattle magazine that had been lying on the coffee table. Prices were, apparently, up in the beef industry. Red Angus cattle were growing in popularity. All along, as he read the magazine, he had been watching Rosie work on her coloring book at the other end of the small table. She was now scribbling furiously and everything on the page in front of her was coming out red and pink.

"What's the picture?" Mark said as he stood and walked over to Rosie. He saw that she had put down a newspaper under her coloring book just like her mother had done for her earlier.

"Good for you," Mark said, pointing at the covering.

Rosie smiled. "I'm coloring a picture for Mommy. She puts them on the refrigerator."

"I'm sure she does," Mark agreed as he looked closer at the page. "Are those flowers?"

"Balloons," Rosie said and then paused before saying softly, "Mommy said a bad word."

Mark wasn't sure he'd heard the girl right. "What?"

"Mommy said a bad word," Rosie repeated, seeming to expect something from him. She was smiling, like she deserved to be praised.

"I don't think your mother said anything," Mark said, frowning. What was she talking about? "I was sitting in the room and I didn't hear anything."

"I heard," Rosie said. Her smile was fading, but she still looked like she was due a bit of praise.

"You couldn't have," Mark said, bewildered. "And keep your voice down so you don't wake your mother."

Rosie looked up at him then and he saw her expression crumble. "You don't want to know the word?"

Her smile was gone and distress filled her face. The girl was starting to cry.

"Look, there's no need for tears," Mark said, feeling helpless as he could see the tears start to roll down her cheeks.

Rosie didn't answer; she just suddenly threw

down her crayon. Then she stood up and ran down the hall to her room.

The sound of running feet must have awakened Bailey because she opened her eyes and looked around. "What's wrong?"

"I don't know," Mark admitted. He could hear the sound of sobs coming from the girl's bedroom. "Rosie and I were sitting here talking about the picture she was coloring. And she said you had said a bad word and I said that couldn't be. You were sleeping. And she started to cry and ran to her room."

Mark felt like a raw recruit who didn't understand even the basic things he should know. "She's still there, crying from the sounds of it."

"Oh," Bailey said like she understood everything. She uncurled herself so she sat straight in the recliner. "I should have talked to her earlier."

"What did I do wrong?" Mark asked.

Bailey put her hands on the arms of the chair in preparation for standing. "Nothing. This is Junior's doing. He made a game with Rosie of 'what did Mommy do wrong.' Mostly it was Mommy said a bad word. But it was his way of asking Rosie to spy on me for him. Rosie didn't understand what he was about, of course. I only know because he told me he was going to catch me in my affair because he was training Rosie to *rat me out*—those were his words."

"Junior did that?" Mark was horrified. His fists clenched without his knowledge. If the man wasn't six feet under, Mark thought, he would hunt him down and tell him what he thought of him. "How could he do that to his own daughter?"

"I'm afraid he didn't have much use for Rosie," Bailey whispered as she finally stood up and steadied herself on the back of the chair. "That's why she wanted to play the game— any game—with him. She got his attention that way. I suppose she thought you'd like the game, too."

Mark shook his head. He was speechless. "I would never."

"She didn't know how you'd feel," Bailey said as she turned to the hallway. "She hasn't known many men. Just Eli. And he wouldn't pay any attention to her either."

"I'm sorry," Mark said. For so many things. For the first time, he wondered if he shouldn't have come back to Dry Creek much sooner. Maybe he could have helped Bailey and Rosie.

"You didn't do anything wrong," Bailey turned and said as she started to walk.

"I didn't do anything right either," Mark muttered to the empty space after Bailey had gone to her daughter's room. He'd always thought that real fathers had some special knowing—that they would instinctively protect their children from heartache. Junior clearly hadn't known a thing about how to treat Rosie. Maybe the biology of fatherhood wasn't all he had thought it was.

Still, Mark was sorry he had disappointed Rosie. He was afraid he'd do it more often if she kept expecting him to fill that father role. A sweet little girl like Rosie should have a daddy like the ones they showed on television.

Just then the timer on the oven went off.

"I'll get it," Mark called out as he stood up and went into the kitchen. At least he knew what to do about a mechanical device like the timer. He turned the buzzer off with a click. Then he took a couple of pot holders from a hook beside the stove and pulled the casserole out of the oven. Everything was bubbling and the cheese had melted and browned. He set the hot dish on the wooden block that was resting on the counter, likely for that purpose. The corn looked ready to cook so he turned the heat on under the small pan.

He had the table set and water in all of the glasses by the time Bailey and Rosie walked into the kitchen. The girl's eyes were red, but she had stopped crying—at least for the moment.

"Everything smells good," Mark said in a hearty voice. Food, he knew, made the day seem brighter for everyone. His troops always felt better after a decent meal.

"And after we eat," Bailey said with a forced cheer, "we're going to practice our tap dance routine. Now that we have the top hat, we're all set. Right, sweetie?"

Rosie looked up and nodded, but she didn't smile.

"She took some lessons in Miles City over the summer," Bailey said to Mark. "She never had a top hat until now though so that will be special. She was the best in the class. Everyone said so."

He noticed Rosie smile slightly when her mother spoke of her success.

"I like to tap," she whispered. "I like the sound my feet make."

"Can I watch?" Mark asked and Rosie glanced up at him shyly. He felt a need to entertain her and he opened his eyes wide as though he'd just thought of something. "But, of course, I'll have to be here. You'll need to use my cane and, without it, I'll be stranded."

Rosie looked at him uncertainly.

He winked at her. "You know, I can walk without my cane, but there's no place I'd rather be than right in the living room watching you."

"We need to be in the kitchen," Rosie said, looking more relaxed. "There's carpet in the living room. No one can do taps on carpet. I need this—" She gestured to the linoleum floor.

Mark hit his forehead and said in an exaggerated voice. "What was I thinking?"

Rosie giggled at that. The sound was fleeting, but the block of regret that was lodged inside Mark melted. He might not be any good at relating to little girls, but at least he wasn't doing any lasting damage.

Bailey and Rosie sat down at the kitchen table and Mark brought the casserole dish and bowl of corn over, and set them in the center of the table.

"We need napkins," Rosie announced happily and she slipped down from her chair and went to a cabinet drawer near the sink. She pulled the drawer open and pulled out a handful of colorful paper napkins.

"Princess," Rosie announced as she placed the crumpled napkins on the top of the table. "Pink ones."

Bailey looked at Mark apologetically and then turned back to her daughter. "I'm not sure Mark will want a—"

Mark interrupted. "Pink princesses are my favorite."

"Really?" Rosie looked at Mark in astonishment.

Mark picked up one of the small napkins and spread it out on the table. "Absolutely. All military men like princesses."

Bailey gave him a skeptical glance.

His eyes twinkled at her. "Diplomatic corps. Very important business. Princesses, you know. They have palace guards."

By that time, he had the napkin firmly settled on his good knee.

"Can I have a palace guard?" Rosie asked, all of her sadness gone now. Her head bounced in excitement. She looked at Mark as though he could make her dreams come true.

"I don't know," Mark said, thinking fast. "As I recall some of the princesses have palace guard dogs. Maybe we could train our new friend to stand duty."

"Poor doggie?" Rosie said skeptically. "He wouldn't know how. He's awfully skinny. And he doesn't even have a name."

"He's eating good," Mark defended the canine. "He'll get stronger every day. And you only need a guard dog for official princess business so he'll have lots of time to get in shape. And he'll have a name by then."

"What name?" Rosie asked.

Mark hated to say he didn't know, but he hadn't given it any thought.

"We'll figure it out soon," he said and that seemed to satisfy her.

Bailey called them to prayer and they all bowed their heads. Bailey thanked God for their day and for the food they were going to eat. Mark decided he could get used to thanking God for the food that he ate. It was only right.

Before long, they had finished eating and Bailey stood up.

"I'll clean up," Mark said as he got up quickly. "You just sit and relax."

"I was only going to gather up what I need to make those cookies," Bailey said as she started to walk toward the cabinets. "They won't take long to stir up."

"I'm the one going to the Bakers," Mark said. "I'm the one who should make the cookies."

Bailey looked at him. "Have you ever made cookies?"

"Well, no, but I've had KP duty in the service," he said. "It was mostly peeling potatoes, but how hard could cookies be? There's not a potato cookie, is there?"

"Not that I know of," Bailey said with an

exaggerated grimace. "I'm not sure the Baker boys would eat them if there was one either. And they'd probably be hard."

"Good," Rosie said forcefully. "Bad boys don't get nice cookies in class."

Bailey looked over at Mark and he turned to smile at her. He was taking the used dishes over to the sink.

"We're not in class," Bailey said, turning back to her daughter. "We want to give them cookies."

Rosie shrugged. "Maybe you could put something besides raisins in the cookies."

"Like what?" Bailey asked. "I don't think we have any nuts. Or dried apples."

"Pickles," Rosie said. "We could put pickles in them."

Before Bailey could even reply, Rosie started to giggle. "Sour pickles."

"I better not see you put anything but love and kisses into these cookies," Bailey said, teasing her daughter with a stern voice.

"Yuckee yuck," Rosie said. "No kisses for any boys."

"What if you have a new baby brother coming?" Bailey asked. "Wouldn't he get any kisses?"

Rosie stood there with her eyes going wide

and then she raced over and planted her lips on Bailey's stomach.

"Kisses for baby," Rosie said.

In an hour, the dishes were done, Mark had finished his laundry and Bailey had the last batch of raisin cookies in the oven.

"Time to practice our taps," Bailey announced as she went out into the laundry room and brought back the portable CD player she and Rosie used.

She brought back a classic tap CD and set it up in the player.

By then Rosie had brought her tap shoes and her new top hat out of her room and was coming into the kitchen.

"Where's Markie?" Rosie asked and the man came out of the laundry room.

"I'm right here," he said as he sat down at one of the chairs at the kitchen table. Then he held out his cane. "You can use this if you want."

Bailey smiled. "I might use it. Rosie needs the shorter one."

Rosie was already putting on her tap shoes.

Mark started to stand, keeping his eyes on Bailey. "You can't be skipping around the kitchen trying to tap with this cane."

He was frowning.

"Why not?" she asked.

"I would think that would be obvious," Mark said. "You can't afford a fall. You can sit and let Rosie dance around you, but that's about all that's safe."

"Spoilsport," Bailey said and then sighed. "You're right, I know."

Over the summer, when Rosie was taking her lessons, Bailey had been able to do the steps with her. Reluctantly, Bailey pulled out a chair from the table and sat down. She was a far cry from where she'd been this past summer.

"You can do the beat for me, Mommy," Rosie called out. She had brought the short cane out from her room and looked adorable in her top hat.

Bailey stood again and walked over to turn on the CD player. She'd already programmed it for the old love song Rosie wanted for her Valentine's Day dance routine. Then Bailey went back to her chair and sat down.

Rosie stood at attention as the music started. She swayed with the rhythm for a few seconds and then she gave a quick twirl with her short cane, angling her foot to take that first critical tap. Within seconds her little girl was flying. Bailey clapped out the beat softly so her daughter could hear. The staccato taps of her daughter's steps hit firm and then they faltered.

Rosie had stopped. "I need help, Mommy. I can't twirl by myself."

Bailey started to rise from her chair. "I can stand—"

"No," Mark said. "I will stand here and help her twirl. You need to stay safely in that chair."

Bailey sat back down. She had to admit she wasn't used to having someone worry about her. She supposed every pregnant woman needed someone to do that. For a second, the image of Emma flashed through her mind. She hoped the young woman had someone who would fuss over her so she didn't fall. Or not eat enough. Or worry herself into the dismals.

Soon the music was absorbing all Bailey's attention and the image of the younger woman faded. Rosie was dancing her heart out, a big smile on her face and her copper-red curls bouncing in time with the song she had chosen—something about two Valentine lovers who couldn't be together and who missed each other on the special day. Bailey didn't know the tune, but it was one that the instructor in Rosie's class had used for some of his lessons.

Everything was going well. Mark seemed to instinctively know when a twirl was needed and he held his hand out so he could steady Rosie in her moment of twirling glory.

Bailey sighed as she saw her old friend gallantly help her daughter twist and turn. No matter what happened next in any of their lives, Bailey knew she would never forget this dance practice. Neither Mark nor her daughter was dressed in their finery, but the expressions of pure joy on each of their faces were perfect. They gave her hope for the future. Maybe having Mark for a friend would be enough for the both of them.

Chapter Ten

Mark had watched Rosie dance until his heart was filled with more pride than a man could rightfully handle. She could grow up to be a genuine star, he figured. He was sure she'd win this contest no matter who else entered. Who else around could have that much talent?

But, he could hardly say any of that to her. Bailey would give him a scolding if he even hinted to Rosie that she was sure to win. And he agreed. It wouldn't be good for the girl to take it all for granted.

He sighed just thinking about it all. And then, he went to the kitchen and put together some food to heat up for his supper.

He was heading back to the bunkhouse so the girl and her mother could have a late-afternoon nap. They both looked exhausted once the excitement of the dance wore off. Mark wasn't sure this much activity had been good for Bailey, but she wouldn't want him to caution her any more than he already did. She'd always been independent, even as a child. Of course, he reminded himself, they had both been that way—they'd had to be to survive.

Snow was coming down hard and the ground was frozen underneath the fat flakes. The light was fading from the day, but it was not yet evening.

Hurrying a bit to get inside the bunkhouse, Mark set the bag of food on the porch so he could twist the doorknob. When he opened the door, he was greeted by an excited bark from the dog and a push of warm air that enveloped him.

"Good doggie," Mark said as he reached down to pat his canine friend. Since the dog didn't immediately go to explore the bag of food, Mark decided that the animal's welcome was for him alone.

Mark closed the door and looked around. The windows in the bunkhouse were layered with white frost and the light bulbs overhead were weak ones, but the place satisfied him. He'd made his home in humbler places around the world. Last night, Josh had pulled the two rocking chairs out of the foreman's suite and settled them in front of the stove so now Mark walked over and sat in one of them.

"Ah," he said as he set the bag down and pulled his wet boots off. Today was a good day and his stockings were thick ones. After a few minutes, he took the bag of food into the foreman's suite next door and put it in the refrigerator.

When he came back into the main room, he looked over to the nightstand by his bed and eyed the pamphlet Mrs. Hargrove had given him. He'd glanced through it when he came over earlier to get his laundry. He'd smiled then because it was about washing away one's sins and he'd just asked himself how he was going to wash away the streak of grease he'd gotten on his jeans when he'd slid under the old tractor in the barn last week. He figured there would be no clue in the pages to answer that particular question, but he did ponder how impossible it would be to get rid of a stain made of one's sins.

Mark sat down in one of the rocking chairs before the fire and wondered if his whole life would be about improving himself now that he was out of the service. When he got tired of thinking about that, he asked himself if Junior had ever thought about his mortality. The man had died without warning. At least Mark's army years had prepared him for the unexpected nature of death. He hoped for Rosie's sake that there really was a heaven and that Junior had a shot at being there. Even if Junior had been an indifferent father, he was glad Rosie had some mild affection for the man.

The heat was making Mark a little drowsy and he decided to close his eyes for a bit while he sat by the stove and relaxed. The dog was nestled at his feet and the wind was blowing outside. Mark was content.

He must have fallen asleep because he was startled when he woke to the sounds of a vehicle driving up the lane. Mark recognized the grinding cough of Josh's pickup and he looked at the clock on the wall. It would not be dark for an hour so Mark figured the weather must be taking a turn for the worse to make Josh come back early.

The man himself was pushing through the door before Mark even decided to get up from the chair.

"Sure is cold out there," Josh said as he shut the door firmly and then stomped the snow off his boots. "And the snow's so heavy you can't tell if it's getting dark because of the time or if the clouds are just crowding out any sun."

"It's probably some of both," Mark said.

"Yeah, I suppose," Josh said as he shook the

snow off his heavy coat and hung it on one of the pegs close to the door.

"Everything good at your uncle's place?" Mark asked, grateful there were two rocking chairs by the fire here so he didn't need to think of leaving his own to let the other man warm himself.

"Good as can be expected," Josh said. "But crowded! Those grandkids of his are terrors! Makes a man want to stay single."

"Yeah, well, kids," Mark said in what he hoped was a sympathetic tone. He never liked to complain about anyone's relatives, but he was happy that Rosie was a delightful child and not like some he had heard about. Suddenly, a thought occurred to him that made him sit up straight.

"You like Rosie fine though, don't you?" Mark asked.

"Sure," Josh said as he settled into the other rocking chair. "She's a good little girl. Obedient."

Mark frowned slightly. He wasn't sure that was the word he'd like used for Rosie. It might hold her back. "She's actually quite exceptional—you should see her do her tap dance routine. The one she's practicing for that Valentine talent show at the café."

"Oh, yeah," Josh said as he pushed a chair a

little closer to the stove. "I heard she was going to enter. She'll do fine."

"She'll do great," Mark said, trying not to scowl at the other man. "She'll win hands down."

Josh looked at him. "Well, sure, I suppose she could."

Mark decided he wasn't as comfortable sitting here in front of the fire as he thought he would be. But Josh was studying him with a speculative look in his eyes so he figured he'd best stay where he was.

The silence made Mark feel awkward.

"Did you ever figure Bailey and Junior would get hitched?" Mark finally asked just to say something.

"No," Josh said as he stretched his stockinged feet out in front of the stove. He was more relaxed now. "I didn't see that coming."

"I'm surprised she did it," Mark confessed. That had been bothering him since he found out she'd married Junior and he might as well admit it. He knew he wasn't the only one who thought it was strange.

"Well, you were gone," Josh said.

"What's that got to do with anything?" Mark demanded. He stopped rocking.

"I'm just saying you weren't here," Josh said patiently.

"Of course I wasn't here." Mark felt his knees go weak. He was glad he was sitting down.

"I always thought she was sweet on you," Josh said. "That's all."

"Oh," Mark said softly.

"Arnold always thought so, too," Josh added.

Mark snorted. "That old man proposed to her the other day. Did you know that?"

"Arnold?" Josh asked with a smile starting on his face.

Mark nodded.

"He always was a romantic," Josh said. "Never figured him for something like that though. What did she say?"

"She didn't say yes, that's for sure," Mark said.

Josh chuckled. "Then what happened?"

"Arnold said I should be the one marrying Bailey," Mark said. "I told him I plan my own life."

Josh nodded. "Then what?"

"I bought those shirts you see hanging in the closet," Mark said. "And the suit, too."

Josh shook his head in what looked like pity. "So you just let your chance slip right through your fingers."

"I'm not a marrying man," Mark said stiffly.

There was no need to pity him. "No sense in being something I'm not."

Josh shrugged. "So what do you figure to do? I know you're worried about her, especially with the baby coming."

"I figured you'd marry her," Mark said.

Josh laughed out loud at that. "I don't get between a man and his woman."

"But Bailey and me...we've never been—" Mark started until Josh held up his hand.

"I was here, remember," Josh said. "She used to come over to the ranch all the time."

"She was tutoring Junior in math," Mark protested. "And then English, I think. And maybe history for a while. For years, she tutored him. The guy wouldn't have made it out of grade school, let alone high school, without her."

"But all those years she was looking at you," Josh countered and then, when he saw Mark's expression, he added. "I have eyes in my head."

They were both silent for a few minutes, listening to the wind blowing outside.

"I noticed you looking at her, too," Josh said.

"Well, I—" Mark stopped. He was going to have to face the issue at some point. "The truth is, I'd give my eye teeth to marry Bailey, but I'm no good at the family stuff. I made Rosie cry today and I came close to having Bailey in tears, too. What would their life be with me?"

"So you're scared?" Josh asked quietly.

"I'm just hoping for better for them," Mark said, suddenly very weary.

Josh didn't seem to have any words to say to that so they rocked together for a good while. By then it was fully dark outside and it was cozy inside the bunkhouse.

"I brought some soup over for us," Mark said. "And some tuna sandwiches. I put them in the refrigerator in that suite over there. We can heat the soup up and be set for supper."

"Sounds good to me," Josh said as he stood up. "I don't mind an early night either. I figure we'll be up before usual to feed the cows if you want to get over to the Bakers by the time you said."

"You heard about that, did you?" Mark asked. He wasn't really surprised. Gossip seemed to keep everyone informed around here.

Josh nodded. "My uncle is good friends with the men in the church. He heard about it before I got over to his place today."

"Well, I guess it is newsworthy," Mark said.

"Dead man walking," Josh said with a grin. "That's you. Least that's what the old men say."

"Well, it's worth a shot to talk to the man,"

Mark said. "Sometimes men just need a little shake-up to get back on the straight and narrow. And tell your uncle and his friends that we'll be safe enough."

Josh nodded and Mark figured they all knew he had military training.

The ranch hands next words dispelled that notion though. "You'll be safe as a baby if you're taking Mrs. Hargrove with you," Josh said. "That woman can stare down a snake and stop him from striking. Then, she'll nag him until he repents of his wicked ways."

"So I've heard," Mark said wryly.

"I'm kind of surprised she hasn't been working on you," Josh said as he walked over to the door that led to the foreman's suite.

Fortunately, Mark thought, Josh walked into the next room without looking back or waiting for an answer. Mark wasn't sure his face wouldn't give him away. He could still hear the sorrow in the older woman's voice as she talked to him. Not that he needed to consider repenting, he assured himself.

He had made himself nervous, Mark thought, so he was reassured to hear the sounds of a metal pan being set on the stove in the other room. Josh was managing their supper fine. All was right with the world. He just needed to roll his shoulders a few times so the tension would leave his neck.

Mark stood up and walked over to the nightstand by his bed where that pamphlet lay. That was the problem. He picked it up and put it in the top drawer. A man needed some privacy if he was going to think about his life. Not that he had to do that right now either.

He was relieved when Josh came back carrying a couple of TV trays.

"The soup is cooking," the ranch hand said as he set a tray next to each rocker.

"Thanks," Mark said. "I'd have had a hard time carrying those trays with my leg like it is."

Josh nodded absentmindedly.

"Which is one more reason why—"

Josh made the stop sign again with his hand. "I don't think Bailey is looking for a pack mule to marry." The other man grinned. "Although you are stubborn enough to be one so maybe that will work in your favor."

Mark tried to scowl, but his lips kept turning up in a smile. "You just wait. Someday you'll be in this situation, too. When was the last time you met a woman you'd like to get to know better?"

Josh's grin faded and his face turned red. "The funeral."

"Eli's funeral?" Mark asked in astonishment. "There weren't any strange women there."

"There was one," Josh said quietly. "With the lawyer. I helped her back to the car when they were leaving. It was starting to snow and it was slick."

"Emma?" Mark asked. "You want to marry Emma?"

"Of course not," Josh said, his voice forceful. "You just asked for one I'd like to get to know better. I'm not marrying anyone. But she looked—" He paused. "She looked interesting."

"A tornado would be interesting," Mark muttered wryly. "A termite invasion would be interesting. The plague was interesting."

"I get the picture," Josh said. "So she's in a predicament. Who hasn't been?"

Mark sputtered for a moment and then he grinned. "You know, I think it would be interesting to watch you get to know Emma after all."

Josh didn't respond for so long that Mark figured that the fun was over. They ate in silence. But when they were finished, Josh cleared his throat.

"I'm sorry if I worried you any with my opinions," Josh said. "I hope it didn't make your PTSD act up."

"I don't think you even know anything about PTSD," Mark said. "I know soldiers who suffer from it and I wouldn't hesitate to ask for help if I needed it. But I don't have it. Period."

"You're sure?" Josh asked.

"Absolutely," Mark said. "The doctors said no."

"Did I spread a rumor about it, then?" Josh asked, his voice muffled.

"Looks like it," Mark said. "But I forgive you."

"Still don't know why you have your dog then," Josh said. "He's a mangy thing."

"The mutt's good company," Mark said, looking over at where the canine was dozing.

Josh snorted. "That animal hasn't moved all day. It was in the same place when we left to go to church. A block of wood is as much company as he is."

"Well, Sunday is a day of rest on the Rosen Ranch," Mark said, trying to keep his voice sounding somber.

"That dog rests so much it might as well be dead," Josh complained. "I liked it better when it was snarling at the church women. At least then it showed some gumption. Why, the mutt doesn't even have a name."

"I'm getting around to naming him," Mark said.

"When are you going to do it?" Josh demanded.

"After you call up Emma," Mark retorted. That ended the conversation.

Mark went to sleep more quickly than he expected that night, but not before he noticed Josh was over in his bunk tossing and turning. Mark wondered if the man really was going to call Emma. Then he wondered what he was going to name that mutt of his.

Bailey woke up the next morning wishing she could stay in bed for a week. Frost lined all of the windows and the air was cold. But she knew Mark was going to go over to see the Bakers today and she felt she should give him a hot breakfast before he went. She had slept in her own bed last night instead of with Rosie. Her daughter was so tired she probably hadn't noticed the difference.

The sun had not come up yet, but it was seven according to the wall clock. Bailey got dressed and went out to the kitchen. She turned the thermostat up and got a carton of eggs out of the refrigerator. There was bacon and it wouldn't take much to make some pancakes.

She turned the radio on low to get the weather forecast and heard the temperatures were going to be higher today than they had been yesterday. The snowplow had cleared the roads, too. It was a good day for a drive.

She looked over to where the plastic container filled with cookies sat. She had four dozen oatmeal raisin cookies and, when she went to bed last night, she figured that was about right for three boys, all under eight. A page from Rosie's coloring book sat on the lid. It was a picture of a warrior princess. The royal dress was pink, but the princess held a sword high. Rosie had added the weapon to the picture. Still, Bailey thought the Baker boys would probably rather see an armed princess than one that was sitting and drinking tea. Or worse yet, sleeping while waiting for the prince to appear.

The bacon was frying and the pancake batter was sitting ready to pour when Rosie came to the doorway into the kitchen.

"Are the Baker boys going to get in trouble today?" Rosie asked. She was still in her pajamas and her hair was going every which way.

Bailey couldn't tell if her daughter was worried or vengeful. She was not happy though. That much was obvious.

"You never did say what the Baker boys did to make you afraid of them," Bailey said softly.

"I'm not afraid of them," Rosie protested. "Billy Baker takes the bows out of my hair and throws them in the air." She paused. "That's not nice."

"He doesn't hit you or trip you or anything?" Bailey asked just to be sure.

Rosie shook her hair, her curls bouncing.

"Billy's the oldest one, isn't he?" Bailey questioned and received a nod. "Do the two younger ones bother you?"

"They laugh when Billy throws my bows up," Rosie said indignantly. "And they're *my* bows!"

"I see," Bailey said. She was going to have to tell Mark that the complaints against the boys were not as bad as they had both suspected. "Maybe I should make a cake to go with the cookies."

There was a knock on the front door then and Rosie raced to answer it. Bailey stepped over to the window. She could see the footprints in the snow that came from the bunkhouse. There were no other prints of man or animal so she knew Rosie would be opening the door to Josh or Mark or, more likely, both of them. A delighted squeal confirmed her suspicions.

She put four circles of pancake batter on the griddle and reached for a bowl to use in cracking the eggs.

"Coffee smells good," Mark said as he stepped into the kitchen. "We saw the kitchen light on and figured you were up."

Bailey could hear Rosie and Josh talking in the living room.

"I'm glad you came early," Bailey said. "I finally asked exactly what the Baker boys had done to Rosie."

"And?" Mark asked the question roughly and she could see him strain his muscles as though readying himself to take care of anything that would be mentioned.

"The oldest Baker boy, Billy, would take Rosie's bow out of her hair and throw it in the air," Bailey reported and then walked back to the stove to flip the pancakes that were cooking.

"That's it?" Mark said as he followed her. "No punching, tripping or other bodily harm?"

Bailey shook her head. "Not according to Rosie. Just taking the bow."

"I did that a couple of times to you when we weren't much older than Rosie," Mark said, with a growing smile. "You used to get really mad, too."

"They were *my* bows," Bailey said firmly.

"We lived through it," Mark said.

"I'm thinking cookies aren't enough to give as a peace offering," Bailey said as she poured more batter onto the griddle.

"Don't underestimate how much boys like cookies," Mark said.

It was quiet for a few minutes and Mark spoke again. "I believe Rosie has an admirer."

"Not a very skilled one," Bailey said as she began cracking the eggs and dropping them in a frying pan.

"Well, Billy's only eight years old, I think," Mark said. "We're going to have to cut him some slack."

"I wonder if Rosie and I shouldn't come with you and Mrs. Hargrove," Bailey said. "Maybe we could surround them with kindness."

Mark chuckled. "Sounds good to me."

A rapid series of footsteps sounded and Rosie raced into the kitchen.

"Josh likes my taps," she announced. "He said he'd vote for me if he was a judge in the contest only he's not a judge." Rosie's smile dimmed. "That means he can't vote."

"He can clap though," Bailey assured her daughter. "That way the judges will see how much he enjoyed your dancing."

"Good," Rosie said as she danced over to the table, sat down in her chair and picked up her fork. "I love pancakes."

Josh followed Rosie into the kitchen and Mark poured cups of coffee for himself and the other ranch hand. Then Mark brought over a glass of milk for Rosie and a glass of orange juice for Bailey.

By the time the beverages were all settled on the table, the eggs were done. Bailey pulled the pancakes and the bacon out of the warming oven. She noticed Mark had found the tin of syrup and set it on the table.

"All set," Bailey said as she started to carry a platter with the food over to the table.

Mark interrupted her after she'd taken a couple of steps. "You shouldn't be carrying anything."

She let him take the platter, noting he was doing pretty good walking without his cane for short distances.

"It's nice to have someone help me now and then," Bailey said as she looked at Mark's back. He was doing his duty, she knew. Military straight and proud. But he was doing that duty willingly. Every woman needed—Bailey stopped. She had forgotten again.

"I keep thinking I should call the lawyer and see if he's been in touch with Emma," Bailey said, fretting a little. "I'm a month or so ahead of her, but she's going to need help soon enough."

It was suddenly absolutely quiet. Even Rosie stopped her chattering as she looked at the two men.

"Josh could take a drive over to Missoula

and check on her," Mark said, sounding so-licitous.

"Oh, she's probably fine," Bailey said as she walked over and took her place at the table. "It might just be one of those stray worries that plague pregnant women. I'll call the lawyer later today. He's probably heard from her that she's staying with her mother or something like that."

"She told me her mother had died," Josh said.

"Oh, when was that?" Bailey asked. She hadn't heard anything about Emma's family, not when they had the meeting with the law-yer and not before that from anyone.

"I helped her walk to the lawyer's car," Josh said, a tic starting to show in his jawline. "At Eli's funeral. The snow was deep and she needed to be careful. She told me then that her mother had died some years ago."

"Well." Bailey had never known Josh to have a nervous tic before. "I'll call when we get back from the Bakers and give you a re-port from the lawyer. Surely she keeps him informed."

Bailey felt good about deciding to check on the other woman. She was blessed to have peo-ple who were helping her. She wouldn't want anyone to face pregnancy alone, especially not someone as young as Emma.

"Let's pray so we can eat," Bailey said and everyone bowed their heads.

"We're grateful to you, Father, and we ask that you keep us safe today. Be with Emma. Be with the Bakers. And be with Mrs. Hargrove," Bailey prayed. "Now we ask you to bless this food to our bodies. We ask in the name of Jesus. Amen."

Everyone ate heartily and then Josh and Mark left to feed the cattle and to move them around in some fashion. Mark had washed the dishes before they left so Bailey decided to do as he suggested and sit in the recliner with her feet up.

There was no point in having all of this willing help if she was going to refuse it. She needed to rest so she'd be able to go with Rosie to the Bakers in a couple of hours. She wasn't sure who she felt the need to protect in the upcoming exchange, but she owed it to her daughter to be there.

She smiled remembering a day almost two decades ago when Mark had stolen a bow out of her hair. Redheads were particularly sensitive about their hair because they got teased. She had been and it sounded like Rosie shared that trait. Both of them made it difficult for boys.

Chapter Eleven

All chatter in the pickup stopped as Mark drove onto the lane leading up to the Bakers' house. Mrs. Hargrove and Rosie were in the backseat and Bailey sat next to him on the passenger side. Josh had stayed at the ranch to do some work in the barn.

Mark almost wished the other ranch hand had come. Josh was handy with a hammer and—between the two of them—they might have been able to repair a few things while they were here. Snow covered everything in sight, but it was clear that most of the fences needed to be fixed. Posts were down and some barbed wire hung on the ground. The main door to the barn was crooked. The barn itself badly needed new paint. Of course, no one could do that in the winter damp.

A few bare trees loomed over the small

frame house, a pale green originally. So much paint had chipped away there that it looked speckled. On the Rosen ranch this would be considered a shack. He'd be surprised if there were more than two bedrooms in the house and those would have to be tiny. He couldn't help but wonder where that uncle slept. Maybe it was lack of sleep that kept the man from doing any work around the place.

The porch roof had a bright blue tarp peeking out under the snow. It was the only thing in sight that looked reasonably new. One of the windows in the house was cracked and partially mended with duct tape.

"At least their pickup seems to be working," Mark commented. There was nothing else positive to say. Someone had driven it this morning because the snow had melted off the roof of the cab. The vehicle had a rim of rust along the bottom of the frame, but it had all its hubcaps and other trim.

"I'm guessing that it belongs to the man who is staying here," Mrs. Hargrove said, her voice not as bracing as usual. "As I recall, the husband took the only vehicle with him when he left."

"That's tough," Bailey murmured.

Mark agreed. In a rural area like this, a family needed a vehicle to even get groceries. And what would they do in emergencies?

"I should have come out to check on them sooner," Mrs. Hargrove said, regret clear in her voice. "I just don't usually drive on the gravel roads in winter. I'm fine on the freeways, but..." Her voice trailed off.

"Don't blame yourself," Bailey said. "I could have driven out here, too. Well, maybe not in the last few months, but earlier."

"We're here now," Mark said. "That's the important thing."

Mark resolved to ask Mrs. Baker if she'd accept some help if he and Josh came back with their hammers and some nails.

"I don't see Billy," Rosie said with her face pressed against the side window.

"The two younger boys are probably here," Bailey said. "But Billy should be in school."

"He's older than me," Rosie agreed as she stopped looking.

"He'd need to have someone drive him into Dry Creek to catch the bus," Mrs. Hargrove said. "With all of this snow, that might not have happened today."

"Someone did drive the pickup somewhere," Mark said.

He already knew that Rosie would have to be taken to the hardware store in Dry Creek to catch the bus this coming fall. It would be kindergarten for her, the girl had proudly told him. He wondered how Bailey would manage that when she'd have the baby to worry about, too. Rural life wasn't always easy.

The curtains in the window nearest the front door moved slightly and Mark knew they had been spotted. He glanced down at the clock in the dash and saw they were five minutes early. He parked the pickup beside the other vehicle.

Then he announced, "Nobody is to walk inside by themselves. Unless I'm wrong, there is ice on the ground under this snow and we don't want any falls."

"But you might fall, too," Rosie said, worry in her eyes.

"My cane helps me balance," Mark told her. "I'm pretty steady."

Mark turned to face everyone. "Now, who wants to be first?"

No one volunteered.

"Rosie shouldn't go until I'm there to see she's—" Bailey said. "I mean until I can help her with her coat."

Mark knew that wasn't what she'd been going to say, but he agreed. He didn't want Rosie to be in there by herself either. Not with those Baker boys around.

"I can go," Mrs. Hargrove said. "It takes me longer than most to get settled anyway so that will work fine."

Mark nodded. He didn't have a better plan and Mrs. Hargrove had her cane for protection. Rosie would be fine with the older woman there.

He wrapped the knit scarf around his ears and stepped out of the cab. Then he slid the driver's seat forward so Mrs. Hargrove could climb out. He folded her arm close to his one side and used the other side to grip his cane. She carried her cane. By the time they got to the door, it was open and a brown-haired slight woman stood there looking anxious.

"Good to see you, Mary," Mrs. Hargrove said graciously.

"I'm glad you came," Mary muttered as Mark guided Mrs. Hargrove into the warmth of the living room and saw her settled on a straight-back chair. The older woman laid her cane on the floor.

"I'll be right back," Mark said to both women and went back out the door.

It didn't take long to escort Rosie and then her mother into the house.

Bailey had carried the cookies with her and, once she was standing inside the door, she handed them to Mary.

"For the children," Bailey said with a smile to the other woman. "I know how boys are when it comes to sweets."

Then Bailey took off her mittens and slipped them in her coat pockets.

"My boys will appreciate them," Mary said with a shy smile. Mark noticed she was pretty when she relaxed. And not as old as he had thought. "I haven't had raisins for a while and the oatmeal raisin ones are their favorites."

"They are Rosie's first choice, too," Bailey said.

Mrs. Baker disappeared into another room with the cookies.

Mark stood on the wide mat by the front door and took off his coat. He could see three small figures peeking out from the back of a darkened hallway. He didn't see the abusive man he'd come to see though.

Mark bent to unbuckle his rubber boots and pried them off. He'd deliberately worn the galoshes because he didn't want to have to walk around in his stocking feet at a stranger's house. It was fine to do that at Bailey's place, but it didn't feel like something he should do here, especially when the man of the house might want to kick him out before long.

"I've got water heating for tea," Mary said as she came back into the living room. "You're welcome to come to the kitchen table and have a cup with us. It'll warm you up quicker than anything else."

"That sounds very nice," Mrs. Hargrove said as she stood and removed her wool coat, then draped it over the back of the chair where she'd been sitting. She left the cane on the floor.

Mark saw Rosie scowling into the dark hallway as the adults headed into the kitchen. She clearly knew what lurked there. He hung back to be sure Rosie didn't get caught up with those boys so that meant Bailey went into the kitchen before him. Mark regretted his actions when he saw the man who was sitting at the table next to Bailey.

She'd only been seconds ahead of him and Rosie, but Bailey looked uncomfortable. This man had his chair so close to her that he was almost sitting on her lap. He wasn't a slight man either; Mark figured he'd do well enough in a fighting unit. His muscles bulged beneath the tank top he wore. A tattoo of a bald eagle sat on the arm that Mark could see. He suspected there were two crossed bayonet rifles beneath the bird.

"Army?" Mark asked the man. He'd seen hundreds of tattoos in that same design. Most of them had a tagline of US Army beneath it. This man's probably did, too, and Mark just couldn't see it.

"What's it to you?" the man demanded, already aggressive. "You one of those guys that don't like the military?"

Mark could see Bailey bristling at the man's question, but Mark couldn't get his tongue in action fast enough.

"He has a Purple Heart," Bailey said forcefully. She had turned to face the man directly. "Don't mess with him."

The man sneered. "What's he going to do? Beat me up?"

"I'm thinking about it," Mark answered. He decided not to sit down since it would take him longer than the other man to get back to his feet. "But I figure there's been enough beating up on people in this house already."

Mary gasped and turned to the man. "Joe, you said Billy fell down. You said you didn't touch him."

The man, who must be Joe, didn't answer. His eyebrows drew together and a frown curled his forehead. He spoke to Mark. "Do what you came to do then and get out of here."

Everyone was silent until Mark heard a rustling behind him. He turned around. The shuffling of slippers was coming from the boys who were trying to sneak into the kitchen.

"Hi, boys," Mark said softly. They reminded him of little birds getting ready to take flight at the first sign of trouble.

"Hello," the tallest of the boys mumbled. The smaller two said nothing.

Mark noticed a purple bruise on the cheek of the older boy who must be Rosie's Billy.

"What happened to your face, Billy?" Mark asked as he took a step closer to the child. The boy took a step away from him and uttered something Mark couldn't make out.

Mark looked back at Joe and saw the flash of guilt in the man's eyes.

"You hit him with your fist or something else?" Mark asked him.

"What kind of a question is that?" Joe muttered, glaring at Mark.

Mark scowled back at him, unwavering and fierce, until finally Joe looked away.

"Kids can be a pain," Joe said, fidgeting.

Something felt off-key to Mark. He looked closer at the other man. He was hiding something. "What happened?"

"Nothing," a thin voice spoke up behind Mark. It was Billy. "I couldn't sleep and I walked into the living room to get a new book the teacher gave me. It was on the shelf. I didn't even turn the lights on so I wouldn't wake him up."

"He startled you?" Mark asked as he turned to Joe.

The man nodded, looking at the floor.

"This happen often?" Mark asked. "Where did you serve when you were in the army?"

The man glanced up. "Iraq."

Mark nodded. The man's voice had been flat. He didn't want to talk about it all. "Some hard times?"

Joe shrugged. "You could say that."

Mark paused and thought a moment. This wasn't playing out like he had thought it would. "Mind if we step outside for a moment?"

"Oh, no," Bailey said, starting to stand. "We want it to stay civil."

"It will," Mark assured her and she slowly sat back down. "We're only going to talk." Then he spoke directly to Joe. "Okay?"

The other man nodded his head.

They both grabbed coats and went out the door. The wind was blowing just as strong as before and flecks of icy snow hit them on the face. They each hunched over and moved close together. Wisps of white air formed with each breath they took.

"You ever talk to a doctor about the flashbacks?" Mark asked.

"What's the point?" Joe said, sounding discouraged. "I knew when I left the service I had a problem. The doctors told me. But I didn't want anyone to know. I keep thinking it would go away if I just keep..." His voice trailed off.

"Just keep what?" Mark probed.

"Just keep getting through the day," Joe said as he looked up. "It's got to get better, don't you think? Mary hired me to do some of the work around this place, but I haven't gotten to it. The noise bothers me. The wind bothers me. I can't rest. I'm no good here, but I don't have any other place to go."

"I could come help you with the work," Mark offered. "Get you caught up some."

Joe shook his head. "You don't know what it does to a man to be useless like this."

The other man looked up and Mark saw the grief and distress in his eyes.

"Maybe I do know," Mark said softly. "I think the first step is to deal with your PTSD. There's got to be a doctor around here who can help you. Even the baby doctor has some tips."

"The baby doctor?" Joe grinned. "You asked the baby doctor about PTSD? That I got to hear."

"It wasn't me that asked," Mark admitted. "It was Bailey, but he checked me out anyway even after I told him that the medics had already done so. And, it's a place to start. He's sure to know other doctors around. And there are some organizations. I can find out the contacts for you. If you're willing?"

Joe nodded. "I've got to do something. Folks might think it's strange if I go see a baby doctor though. I wouldn't want anyone to think it was because of Mary. She's not sleeping with any man—says she's still a married woman."

Mark thought about that. He had figured her husband had filed for divorce after he'd left, but he didn't know.

"Maybe you can go with Bailey and me some time," Mark said.

"I could do that," Joe said.

"It'll have to be soon," Mark said. "Bailey doesn't have much time left."

"Sure doesn't look like it," Joe agreed.

"And you were flirting with her?" Mark said indignantly, remembering his grievance.

Joe shrugged. "I thought it would make her feel good. Flattered, you know."

"Well, it didn't." Mark slapped the man on the back. He wasn't going to stand outside and argue about that. "Let's go back inside. It's cold out here."

Joe nodded again. "You're not going to tell everyone are you? About the PTSD?"

"Not unless I have to," Mark said. "But I know for a fact the old men around here—the ones in the church—will be supportive. They'll be eager to help. One might even have useful information on doctors or programs. In fact, I'm sure he'll help. He has a nephew with it.

You'll want to tell Mary first though. She deserves to know."

"She deserves more than that," Joe muttered. "She's put up with a lot… I've been keeping my eye out for a husband for her. He'd have to be someone special though and I haven't met anyone around here good enough."

"I know how that goes," Mark said as he opened the door.

Both men ducked in as quickly as they could. The warmth felt good, but Mark was as cheered by the gentle sound of Bailey talking as he was the heat. He was glad to know what Joe's problem was. At least, he would know how to help him.

Bailey sat at the table while the boys counted raisins. Apparently, to be fair, they each needed to have the exact same number of raisins. It seemed too intense to be a game, but even Rosie was caught up in the counting.

Then Rosie reached out a hand and plucked a raisin from the stack next to Billy.

"Hey," the boy protested.

Rosie just smiled and put the raisin in her mouth. "All of the raisins were mine before the cookies were even made."

"Rosie!" For the first time it dawned on Bailey that her little girl might not be as innocent in all of this bickering between her and Billy Baker as she made others think. "You will need to give Billy one of your raisins now and say you are sorry."

"Sorry!" Rosie protested. "He stole the bows out of my hair and no one made him say sorry."

For the first time today, Bailey noticed that Rosie had not one, but two bows in her hair, one on each side of her head. And they were the black velvet ones with the diamond sparkles in the middle. The bows that were her very best.

A deep chuckle sounded from the doorway and Bailey looked up to see Mark and Joe standing there, grinning.

While she was staring at the men, she heard a gasp beside her and turned to see that Billy had snatched one of the bows out of Rosie's red hair and was holding it high like a trophy. Before Bailey could even speak, Billy was racing out of the kitchen with the bow and Rosie was right behind him vowing she'd catch him and make sure he was sorry.

Mark looked at Bailey, his eyes warm and twinkling, and asked, "Should I go rescue Billy?"

"You might have to," Bailey said. She could already hear screams of laughter coming from some room in the back as Mark and Joe took off down the hall.

"Oh, dear," Mary said, shaking her head. "I try to get the boys to act like gentlemen and this is what happens."

"I guess it's the same as getting girls to act like ladies," Bailey said with a smile. "It's impossible."

"And not a bad thing," Mrs. Hargrove added. "Kids need a little freedom to be young." The older woman turned to Bailey. "I remember when you and Mark were that age. I knew he was going to be all right when he started snatching your bows."

"I don't see how," Bailey said.

"He was connecting," Mrs. Hargrove said with a smile. "He didn't have words, but he was reaching out to you."

Bailey wasn't sure about that, but she accepted the older woman's words. She didn't always understand Mark. That much was a certainty. She knew for sure she didn't know what was going through his mind when he invited Joe to come over to the ranch and bunk with him and Josh for a few nights. She supposed he wanted the other man away from the boys and Mary, but Joe didn't give him a hard time about going. He even nodded when Mrs. Hargrove invited Joe, Mary and the boys to church this coming Sunday.

They all got back to the ranch around noon

and Josh made grilled cheese sandwiches and tomato soup for everyone. Bailey promised to roast a pork loin for the evening meal and everyone was content although Mark did say he'd make the meal under her instructions.

The sun was shining by the time they got up from the table and it was clear that the day was growing warmer. Rosie wanted to go outside and play with the poor doggie and Mark said he'd take her out and stay with her. Bailey knew he wouldn't let any harm come to Rosie and so she nodded her approval. She certainly couldn't take Rosie outside to run around.

Life, Bailey concluded, was settling into a comfortable groove. She was relying on Mark too much. She knew that. But she didn't have the energy to worry about it now. After the baby was born, she would get her life in order. As for right now though, she was going to take a nap.

She'd left her door to the napping room open so she'd hear Rosie if needed, but she went to sleep quickly. She was only half-aware when a downy blanket drifted down on top of her sometime later. She started to wake a little more when a kiss brushed across her forehead, but she finally decided it was Mark. He made her feel safe and she drifted back to sleep.

Chapter Twelve

It wasn't snowing Wednesday so Mark decided it was a good day to separate the cows into groups by age and whether or not they were pregnant. He and Josh did their best to guess which cows would give birth first and they put them in pens closest to the barn.

The gray morning clouds had burned off by midday and they both heard the sound of a pickup driving up the lane. It pulled up close to the barn and Joe stepped out.

"You're a fruitful ranch," Joe said after he walked over and leaned on the main corral fence. He was eyeing the cows. Mark and Josh had moved most of the pregnant ones into that holding.

"Not as fruitful as we'll be next year," Josh said proudly as he put one of his elbows on a sturdy post. "This is good ranch country."

Mark was silent. He wouldn't be here next year. Josh at least had a job long term. Mark's time would be up whenever the requirements of the will were met. He best do more than talk to Mr. Durham about places to buy around here or he'd be homeless.

"The Bakers never had any animals," Joe said as they stood there. "We were lucky to get a big crop of potatoes this past summer."

Mark frowned. "How is Mary making it over there?"

There was no market around for potatoes and he guessed she grew them solely for the family table.

Joe was silent for a minute. "I use my disability check to buy groceries. We don't talk about it. I just go to town and get groceries and leave them on the counter or hide them in the freezer."

"Boys that age eat a fair bit," Josh offered.

Joe nodded. "We manage."

With that Joe turned and began to make his way to the bunkhouse. The drifts were melting and there was more mud than snow around. Mark and Josh stood there and watched the other man go. Joe had left his pickup parked by the barn.

"He's got some surprises to him," Josh finally said.

Mark nodded. "Seems like he slept better last night, too. There might be hope for the guy."

"He doesn't drink," Josh added. "I've kept a watch for bottles and such. Even looked in that pickup of his to see if there were any empties."

"Find anything?" Mark asked.

"He does the crossword puzzles they put in that shopping paper out of Miles City," Josh said. "Pretty good at it, too."

Mark frowned. "He doesn't strike me as an educated man."

Josh shrugged. "Maybe Mary does them."

"And leaves them in the pickup?" Mark asked. "It sounds like the only time she goes anywhere is once in a while to church—and I think someone else gives her and the boys a ride on Sunday."

Josh thought a bit. "Well, I couldn't say."

"Maybe he gives someone else rides," Mark offered.

They turned back to their work in the corral.

Lunch was leftover sandwiches in the bunkhouse and, since the afternoon was growing warmer, Mark let the dog come out into the yard with them. Rosie wanted to come outside, too, and her mom dressed her warm once Mark said he'd keep an eye on her.

As it turned out Joe was playing fetch with

the dog and Rosie joined in. Leaving them to their game, Mark and Josh went back to the corrals to finish their task for the day.

In a couple of hours, Mark noticed that the game of fetch had changed into serious pet training.

Rosie called him over before he even got close to the house to see how she could raise her hand and make the dog growl.

"Good doggie," Rosie said as she patted the mutt's head. The dog looked up at her in adoration. The canine had been given several baths by now and Mark noticed that the dog's hair was brown with copper overtones. He no longer worried about the canine turning on the girl. He was more worried about the dog attacking Billy if the boy ever ruffled Rosie's feathers again.

"You don't want the doggie to hurt anyone," Mark told the girl.

"He's my guard dog," Rosie said proudly. "If someone tries to kidnap me, doggie will stop them. Off with their heads." She made a dramatic gesture across her own neck.

Mark heard a muffled chuckle and looked over at Joe. The other man was trying to keep a straight face.

"I tried explaining limited response," Joe said. "It didn't take."

"I'm not surprised," Mark said as he turned to Rosie. "You can have him growl if there is a kidnapping. Or have him come find me. But you're not to make the dog think that someone is hurting you when they are not. If it's just play, don't go screaming for the dog."

Rosie reluctantly nodded. Mark wondered if she was bloodthirsty or if she just didn't understand what would happen if the dog bit someone.

"Who should I scream for if I can't scream for my dog?" Rosie asked. Mark noted she was practical like her mother.

"Me," he said. "You can scream for me."

That made Rosie happy enough and she turned to walk back to the house.

The dog watched her go, but Mark noted the mutt didn't seem forlorn. The beast was content to stay there with the three men.

Mark bent over and patted the dog. "We need to give you a name, Old Boy, don't we?"

The canine leaned into Mark's leg, probably in hopes of getting scratched. Mark obliged him.

"How do you feel about Scout?" Mark asked. He'd been thinking of names.

"How about Sarge?" Joe suggested. "If he's going to be a guard dog, he needs some authority."

Mark noted that Joe was talking more about his army days since he'd become comfortable around Josh and him. Mark had set up an appointment with the baby doctor in Miles City for next Monday. He planned to go with Joe even if Bailey couldn't. The physician said he knew of programs and would do a consultation for Joe at no charge. Just having some hope seemed to make Joe do better. He went over to the Bakers early every morning to get Billy off to meet the school bus. Then he drove back to the Rosen ranch until school was over. He picked Billy up and went to the Bakers for a couple of hours before coming back to the bunkhouse for the night.

Josh and Mark went back to working with the cattle. By late afternoon, Mark realized he'd been hearing Rosie's voice for some time. When he walked back toward the house, he saw that Joe was helping her teach the dog more tricks.

Everything seemed quiet around so he thought he'd go inside and see if he could help Bailey with dinner. If he could make it happen, he'd have her take one long nap until the baby came. Of course, Bailey wouldn't stand for that. He'd only bribed her to rest so much today by saying that she'd want to be able to go to the Valentine talent show on Friday. The whole ranch would close down to go see that.

Friday morning, Bailey snuggled into the cocoon of her covers. She felt sluggish and had for several days now. She guessed it was because, for the first time in years, she felt all of her responsibilities lifted from her shoulders. Mark was looking after Rosie. The girl had been bubbling with enthusiasm when she poked her cold nose into the bedroom yesterday afternoon. Full of stories about how she was teaching her dog tricks, Rosie was content. Bailey didn't even need to worry about feeding everyone. Mark and Josh had a handle on that. Even Joe seemed willing to help around the kitchen.

It was nice to not need to worry about anything, Bailey told herself as she lifted her head and looked at the clock on her bedside stand. The numbers told her it was nine o'clock. It would have to be morning because the sun was coming in along the sides of her blinds.

Finally, she realized it was Friday morning. The talent show was going to happen at two o'clock this afternoon. She was going to have to get up and get dressed. She felt a twinge race along her lower back when she lifted herself into a sitting position on the edge of the bed.

It was Valentine's Day and she was going to wear her black pleated top with a big red heart pin that Rosie had made in Vacation Bible school this past summer. She wondered if Mark would recognize the pin. Both of them had made similar pins when they were a few years older than Rosie and in the same Vacation Bible School program. Bailey had given her red heart pin to Mark and he gave a green heart to her. She was hurt, assuming he thought she was jealous or greedy or some such thing. But he never said when she asked. There were so many things he'd never told her, she thought, as she stood up. Of course, they both had unusual upbringings. Maybe by now they would agree on appropriate Valentine Day sentiments. Everyone knew a red heart meant affection.

Chapter Thirteen

Mark saw the red heart pinned to Bailey's black blouse before she even put her coat on and he smiled. He'd be embarrassed if she knew he still had the heart that she'd given him all of those years ago. He'd never had nerve enough to wear it, but it was carefully wrapped in a handkerchief and lying at the bottom of the trunk he'd kept with him throughout his years in the military. The trunk was now stowed at the foot of his bed in the bunkhouse.

"Remember these?" Bailey asked. She must have seen him looking at the pin. "Rosie made it."

"Some things don't change," Mark said with a smile as he watched Bailey finally get her coat bundled around her. She couldn't button it shut and he knew it would not keep her warm enough, but it would help. "Mrs. Hargrove and her hearts."

"You made my heart green," Bailey said accusingly just like she'd done when he gave it to her twenty years ago. "I am not a jealous person."

"It was never about that," Mark replied sheepishly. "It was because green is for go and red is for stop. I wanted your heart to go on and on forever. I didn't know a Valentine heart needed to be red."

"Oh. That was sweet," Bailey said as she stood there. "I wish I'd known that back then. You should have told me."

Mark snorted in disbelief. "What seven-year-old boy is going to tell you that?"

"I suppose you're right," Bailey said, looking a bit sad.

Mark knew Rosie could come barreling into the living room at any moment, but he didn't care.

"I still want your heart to go on and on forever," he whispered, stepping closer and leaning over to pull the collar up on her coat. When he finished getting the coat just right, he glanced down and noticed Bailey looking at him wistfully.

"I want you to be warm, too," he said and then dipped his head to kiss her. He didn't plan for it to be more than a quick tribute to the past, but he found he couldn't stop himself. The past wasn't enough. Everything he'd wanted today and for his future was wound up in that kiss. And then he heard quick footsteps coming from the hall.

"I think I'll be warm forever," Bailey said softly before she turned to greet her daughter.

Mark stood there feeling like he needed to go back to basic training. He didn't understand the kinds of emotions he was feeling. He was supposed to be immune to these things. The kiss was one thing. But the longing that welled up in him wasn't good. He wasn't meant for this kind of life. He wasn't a family man. He needed to stop kissing Bailey.

"Markie!" Rosie's voice pulled him out of his thoughts. She was twirling around in a white-and-black velvet dress with a full skirt that flared out with a dozen net petticoats. Her black patent leather shoes shone. Her copper curls shimmered and her black velvet bows sparkled.

"You look like a princess," Mark said in awe.

The girl giggled and clapped her hands. As if on a signal, the dog came out from the hallway wearing a black velvet bow around its head and glitter sprinkled over its back. The dog came right up to Rosie and seemed to sit at attention.

Mark smiled. Rosie finally had her partner. He'd be sure and stand beside them so he could help her do her twirl, but she looked confident and ready.

Josh came inside then and whistled at Rosie, to her delight.

"Oh," Bailey said, like she just remembered something. She went over to the small table that held the phone and picked up a piece of paper. Then she turned to Josh. "I finally got a call back from the lawyer about Emma. He's a little worried, too. Here's his number. I'm hoping you can go check on her in the next few days. She's probably fine, but I'd feel terrible if—"

Josh interrupted before Bailey finished. He walked over and accepted the paper from her hand. "I'd feel bad, too. I'll leave after the talent show."

"But you won't have time to drive there and get back today," Bailey protested. "And it's getting colder. I wouldn't be surprised if it's snowing before the end of the day. Maybe you should wait for tomorrow."

"I've got an uncle who lives close to Missoula," Josh said and glanced over at Mark. "A different uncle than the one here. We're a big family." Josh turned back to Bailey. "Anyway, I've got time to get over there today even if I wait until after the show. That way I'll be back tomorrow afternoon with my report on how she's doing."

"I'd appreciate it," Bailey said. "I know she's probably got family over there, but—"

Mark nodded to Josh. He was glad the other man was going to check, as well. If the lawyer was worried, Mark was too. Unlike Bailey, he didn't think having family was always enough.

Everyone needed to do a few last-minute things before they were ready to head off to the café for the talent show. Josh packed a small duffel and got his pickup ready for his longer drive to Missoula later. Mark changed into his new suit and then brought the ranch pickup close to the house for Rosie, Bailey and, of course, the dog.

"Don't forget the music," Rosie called out to her mother as they both walked toward the door to go outside.

Rosie was carrying her top hat and her cane. Mark reached out to take the portable CD player out of Bailey's hands.

"It's enough if you carry your purse," Mark told Bailey.

"The CD is in the player," she said as she handed it over. "I just checked."

Mark carefully led each one to the pickup, starting with Rosie. He even carried the dog since Rosie had spent hours combing the mutt's hair. Bailey was his final passenger.

Mark concentrated on the road as he drove into Dry Creek. Bailey was right about the changing weather. The skies were growing grayer as time went on. The air felt damp, too. Given the low temperatures, that probably meant some snow before the day played out. He was glad that the talent show was scheduled for midafternoon instead of evening.

When Mark pulled up to the café, he counted over twenty pickups scattered around the building; some parked on the street and some found a place in the wide space between buildings.

There was always a heavy dark blanket in the backseat of the pickup and Mark wrapped it around Rosie as he hauled her into the café. The burst of warm air was comfortable, but he left immediately to go back and get Bailey. This time, he decided, the dog could get his feet wet and wait next to the café in the large enclosure reserved for animals.

When Mark came to the door the second time, Mrs. Hargrove was there and opened it for him and Bailey. The scent of coffee drifted toward them. Mark hadn't been in the café for years and it looked better than ever to him, despite all of the people inside. A door led to the kitchen in back. Various people were sitting at round tables that had been pushed to the walls. Black-and-white linoleum covered what floor was visible. Large red hearts hung from the ceiling and twisted in the air. A red-topped counter ran along the left wall. And, on that counter, were dozens of heart-shaped boxes of candy ready for sale.

Dry Creek was going all out for this day.

"Wow," Mark said in admiration. He liked that these ranchers and their wives took time to celebrate.

"The day is finally here," Mrs. Hargrove said with a smile as she nodded her head at Rosie. The girl was chattering and laughing and having a grand time with another young girl. "Time for the contest."

"She's been practicing," Mark said.

"So has her friend Lucy," Mrs. Hargrove replied. Then she gestured to a small table beside the door. "There's punch and cookies before the show if you want some."

Mark nodded and glanced down at Bailey. She was looking around the crowded eatery, probably to see who was there. As far as Mark could tell, half of the people in the county were there. He saw Josh talking to some of the ranchers and decided to move over there.

Before he got there though he was walking alongside the counter with the heart-shaped candy boxes. He wondered if he should buy one for Bailey. Women set some store by such gestures, he believed. There were so many red hearts and a few gold ones. They all had extravagant bows and some had silk flowers attached.

He looked up and noticed that Josh was watching him, amusement lurking in his eyes.

"Just looking," Mark said as he finished walking past the hearts and made his way to the other man. When he got there, he looked up nonchalantly. "Thought you might want to buy one for Emma."

"Me?" Josh protested. "I barely know her." His face flushed. "Besides, I thought about buying her some groceries before I get to her place. I think she'd like that better than some fancy box of candy."

"You may be right," Mark conceded and then grinned. "Although nothing says 'I'd like to get to know you' more than a big box of chocolates."

Josh snorted. "What do you know about it?"

"Nothing," Mark agreed airily. "But I might buy a box all the same."

Mark saw the owner of the café and signaled her to set aside one of the boxes for him. "A big one," he mouthed and she nodded.

Mark was distracted then because he saw Gabe walk into the café and walk over to Rosie. He patted the girl on the head and appeared to be wishing her well in the competition. He guessed maybe the man did view Rosie and Bailey as family, after all.

Gabe walked over to him and said, "I'm having trouble finding that Amber Cast Iron company that Eli wanted for the bell tower. I'm not giving up though. I have some people to ask."

"Good," Mark said with a nod.

Gabe walked away and, a few minutes later people started to move to the edges of the café, some of them sitting on a chair and some of them leaning against the wall. Mark managed to snag a chair by the door for Bailey and motioned her over.

Gradually the movement and rustling settled down and Linda Enger, the long-time owner of the store, stepped into the middle of the empty space and lifted a small microphone up.

"Happy Valentine's Day, everyone," she said and people cheered. "I'm glad to see all of you here for our annual youth Valentine talent contest. We have six entrants today and we wish them all well as they perform. Remember, the grand prize is a hundred-dollar gift card and a Valentine box of the winner's choice." At that, the woman gestured to the lineup of heart-shaped candy boxes.

A boy of ten years old juggled five balls for two minutes while whistling. Mark applauded him heartily. Then a teenage girl sang the national anthem and hit most of the notes right. He applauded her, too, mostly for her courage. The youngest two Baker boys played a song, one on a guitar and the other on drums. Mark looked around and saw Joe standing with Mary and Billy as they cheered on the two boys. An older boy performed some magic tricks, pulling a penny out of many unexpected places. Rosie's friend was up and she played a delightful song on a flute.

Then it was Rosie's turn to shine. Bailey had the CD ready to go and Rosie had already let the dog inside so she called him over from his place by the door. Mark stood up, far enough away from Rosie so he wouldn't interfere but close enough that he could close in when she needed a hand for her twirls. Before she started, Rosie stroked the dog's back so his hair was tidy.

Mark looked around, but didn't see anyone who even recognized the dog now that the beast was well-groomed. The music started and Rosie struck a pose, her cane in her hand and her top hat on her head. For a second, Mark thought she looked like a red-haired Shirley Temple with her curls and her impish smile.

Then the beats started and Rosie began to tap. Her toes tapped, her heels tapped, the cane tapped. Even the velvet bow clipped into her mass of hair quivered in time to the music. And then Rosie held a hand out and Mark stepped in to help her execute a twirl. Which only set her off on another whirlwind of taps and flying feet. Mark noticed the dog was inching in closer to Rosie, glitter falling off his back like fairy dust.

Rosie held out her hand for Mark to hold and she gave a magnificent final twirl. People were standing up to applaud when Rosie slowed down enough to take a solemn bow. That made people clap louder and then she motioned for the dog to come to her and she signaled the animal to cross his front legs, with his hind end in the air, and dip his head. Mark was amazed that the dog could bow like that, but the canine seemed to enjoy it.

Mark looked over at Bailey and they shared a proud moment. He never thought he'd be so touched by a child's efforts, but he was. Rosie was special to him.

* * *

Bailey was thrilled. She supposed every mother wanted their child to be a star at something and this was Rosie's day. Bailey watched as her little girl got even more applause and bowed yet again.

And then Linda was walking to the center of the area again with her microphone.

"The judges will step into the kitchen for a few minutes and compare our votes," the café owner said. "So have some more punch and tell someone you love them. We'll be out before you know it."

Linda and several others headed off to the kitchen. Bailey sat right where she was. Her feet were still tapping, but she was settled. Her chair by the door was one of the best seats in the house she thought as she saw Mark walk over and study those heart-boxed candies. She wondered who he had in mind to give one of those to. Not, she supposed, that it was any of her business. Just because she'd been friends with him her whole life didn't mean she should crowd him. She looked around quickly. There weren't really any single women around anyway. Well, except for her and maybe Mary Baker. Although Mary was apparently still married.

The judges came back into the main area and Linda picked up the microphone again.

"Our winner today is Rosie May Rosen!"

Bailey stood up without thinking about her back and her swollen ankles. Her little girl had won. Bailey joined in the applause with her whole heart before she felt a pain race across her abdomen. Her backache had returned. She figured she might feel better if she stayed on her feet for a few minutes.

She saw her friends and neighbors surge forward to congratulate Rosie. The Bakers were there first, then Josh, the minister, some of Rosie's classmates, Mrs. Hargrove and several local ranchers.

Then Josh walked by her carrying the heart-shaped box of candy that Mark had been admiring. Josh nodded to her and mouthed "Missoula." She nodded in response, glad Mark was sending the candy along. Josh would probably say it was from everyone on the Rosen ranch and that would be a nice thing to give the young woman.

Josh opened the door and the cold air rushed in. He closed it behind himself, but it seemed people were starting to leave and a minute later there was another blast of winter. She was almost going to look for another place to stand when she heard a familiar screech from inside the crowd of people in the middle of the room.

"Rosie!" she called.

Then she saw Billy Baker running past her with Rosie's black velvet bow held high in his hands like a trophy. The door was open as someone else was leaving and Billy started to race through. Then Bailey heard the low growl from the dog and, almost immediately, a dark shape raced after the boy.

"No-o-o!" Bailey cried. That dog was going to bite the boy. Without thinking, she knew she needed to stop that dog. She rushed to follow the mutt out the open door, moving as fast as she could, and took a step off the porch as she watched the boy wind between two pickups. The dog was tearing after him.

"Bailey," she heard Mark call, but she didn't turn back. She was focused on what was ahead.

"Come back," Bailey breathlessly pleaded with the dog as she tried to catch up. Someone really needed to name that beast, she thought, as her foot went down wrong on a slick place and, before she even knew what was happening, she hit the ground. Shooting pain went through her like lightning. She'd turned mid-air so she would fall on her side and now she curled up as best she could. Then she knew nothing more as her mind went black.

Chapter Fourteen

Mark's heart had stopped. He'd heard Rosie call out and saw the dog chase Billy Baker out of the café. It wasn't until he was at the door that he realized Bailey had gone after them. He called, but she hadn't turned back. Then she fell and here he was, forcing himself down to the frozen ground to try to figure out how she was. His cane had gone to the snow near him. Fortunately, he and Bailey were sheltered between two parked pickups so the cold wasn't so bad.

He couldn't think. He felt for Bailey's pulse and was relieved to find it beating strong. He gently felt around her head and pulled a hand back in alarm when he discovered he had blood on it. She'd hit the ground forcefully. She probably had a concussion. Then he felt her body squeeze in upon itself and he remembered the baby.

"Help!" he called, so focused on Bailey he hadn't realized that half of the people in Dry Creek were already gathered around.

Josh separated himself from the pack and came close. "What do you need?"

"She hit her head," he said. "I don't know if she can be moved. Do you know if anyone around has a gurney?"

"I have a stretcher I use sometimes for calves," one of the ranchers in the back said. "I made it myself. It should do for a person, as well. I'll get it—it's in my pickup."

The rancher took off at a fast clip.

Mark was starting to sweat. He needed to remember everything he read from that pregnancy book. Not that Bailey was going to have the baby now, he assured himself as he felt along the sides of her stomach. But he needed to be careful they didn't do anything to damage the baby while they were helping Bailey.

Lord, help me. The words came unbidden to Mark's mind. He'd been reading that pamphlet from Mrs. Hargrove at night, but he still wasn't lined up with everything it said. It all fell into place now though. He needed God.

"Here," the rancher, clearly winded, held out a small stretcher.

Mark took it and tested it. It was sturdy.

"I need to get her to the hospital," Mark said.

She'd fallen on her left side and Mark felt along her spine, praying as he went and paying particular attention to her neck area. "Anyone know about spine injuries?"

He looked up, hoping someone had medic training. He was surprised when Joe stepped forward. "I've done triage more times than I'd like to count. Mostly explosions, but we had some spine injuries from the falls."

As the man spoke, he was stepping closer and finally crouched down beside Bailey and Mark. Joe ran his hands down Bailey's spine, too, and finally nodded.

"No breaks," he said. "We'll still want to lift her careful."

"You're sure?" Mark asked.

Joe nodded. "We can't leave her lying in the snow. The blizzard is starting to turn colder and she'll get frostbite and then—"

Joe left the rest unspoken, but Mark did not need to be told. There was no time to wait for an ambulance to get here from Miles City. Someone—and it had to be him—had to make a decision.

"Lord, please," he mouthed the words. He had never felt so helpless in his life. He wasn't entitled to ask for divine help, but he knew God cared about Bailey. Everyone cared about her.

And then Gabe pushed his way through. "I called from inside and the medevac helicopter will be here in ten minutes—maybe sooner."

"I didn't know they had something like that," Mark said, looking up at his old child-hood enemy. Relief poured through him.

Gabe nodded. "It's new."

"Thanks," Mark said, silently taking back every bickering word he'd ever said to Gabe.

"She's my family, too," Gabe said as he stood there looking like he felt as useless as Mark. Then he perked up. "I'll drive Mrs. Har-grove and Rosie in. It'll take us longer, but they only let one person go in the helicopter."

Mark knew that was him. "Me."

Gabe nodded. "I think she'd want you with her."

"Anyone have any blankets?" Mark asked the collection of people around him. "We need to keep her warm."

Mark took his coat off and put it around Bailey. Then several of the other men did the same thing. Finally, a rancher's wife stepped up then with several blankets. "We keep some in our pickup."

Mark put a tower of blankets around Bailey and she stirred, moving slightly and moaning.

"Bailey? Honey?" Mark murmured, but she didn't answer.

Suddenly, he heard the faint sound of helicopter blades and looked up into the sky. Dark clouds were to the west, but he could see the lights of the helicopter flying below them.

"They're coming," Mark said, in relief. Then he looked around. "Get some of these pickups out of here so they can land."

A handful of men took off to get to their vehicles and move them.

The helicopter landed smooth and a medical person of some sort jumped down from the side door and came loping toward where Mark and Bailey were.

"Her pulse is strong, but she hit her head," Mark said as the man came close enough to hear. "And she's very pregnant. I'm worried—"

By that time, the medic was running his hand over Bailey's back and examining the gash on her head.

"It was good that she fell on her side," the man said with a quick reassuring look at Mark. "You're the husband?"

"Friend," Mark corrected him and saw the medic look at him with a little less friendly eye.

"One of those 'significant other' deals?" the man said as the helicopter pilot joined the group, holding a regular gurney.

"Let's get her loaded up," the pilot said. "This blizzard isn't getting any better."

The medic and the pilot loaded Bailey on the gurney quickly.

"Coming?" the medic looked back at Mark.

Mark nodded. "Absolutely."

Then he tried to get up from the ground and realized he couldn't. His cane had been buried under snow someplace close. He wasn't even sure he could get upright with his cane. He'd crawl to that helicopter if he had to though.

Gabe must have seen the problem because he stepped close. "Grab my arm."

With the other man's help, he was able to stand upright. Someone else saw his cane and dug it out of the snow.

"Here," the man said as he held the cane out.

"Thanks." Mark took the cane and turned to go to the helicopter.

"I'll be there shortly with Mrs. Hargrove and Rosie," Gabe called out as Mark moved as fast as he could. The medic gave him a hand to hold on to as Mark climbed into the helicopter. And then they were off.

Bailey felt like she was flying, but that was impossible. Unless she was a butterfly. Maybe that was it. She felt a warm cocoon all around her. Then she heard the sounds of voices and decided that couldn't be right either. She tried to listen closely, but it sounded like someone was praying. That couldn't be right either since it was Mark's voice. It must be a dream she finally concluded. A soft, floating dream.

And then the pain hit her. Something was wrong. The baby.

"Dear Lord," she whispered and felt someone take her hand. It was Mark; she couldn't see him, but she knew it was him. He was here.

"Please, Lord," he whispered, too, and then he kissed the back of her hand.

She gripped his hand even tighter. And then the blackness claimed her again.

Chapter Fifteen

They wouldn't allow Mark into the examination room where they took Bailey. He wasn't her husband, they said, and he had no papers showing he was the person she wanted notified of medical issues. They would not take his word for anything. He could sit in the waiting room, they said, and they would give him some information when they could. It suddenly seemed to Mark that it had been a grave oversight on his part not to marry Bailey before something like this could happen.

How was he supposed to breathe if he didn't know that she was okay?

He paced the floor of the waiting room a couple of times, no doubt annoying the only other occupant—an elderly man who kept tapping his fingers against the side of his chair. The one place Mark didn't go was a portioned-off area for children and he could see it was empty.

When Mark saw Gabe enter the room from the hall, he walked as fast as he could to his childhood enemy and hugged him.

"You're a lawyer, right?" Mark asked after he stepped back. He told himself Gabe had no reason to look so shocked. Men hugged each other from time to time. Maybe not the two of them, but—

"I am." Gabe nodded cautiously. "Why?"

"You can fix it so they'll tell me all about Bailey's condition," Mark said, feeling better already.

"I'm afraid I can't do that," Gabe said. "You have to be family. They won't make an exception."

Mark thought a moment. "Tell them I plan to marry her. That should be enough. Don't you think?"

"Not really," Gabe said. "The only one of us that they could even tell would be Rosie."

"Rosie?" Mark reared back. "They wouldn't tell a child."

"Probably not," Gabe agreed. "But legally she is the only family Bailey has. By bloodline, you know. Rosie and Mrs. Hargrove will be here in a minute. They stopped at the restroom."

They were silent as they waited. Then Mark started to pace the floor again.

A nurse came through the door of the waiting room and Mark's heart leaped, but she directed some comments to the elderly man and he followed her out of the room.

Mark kept pacing. When he passed Gabe the second time, Gabe spoke. "So, are you going to?"

"Going to what?" Mark asked.

"Marry Bailey," Gabe said.

"How can you even think about that at a time like this?" Mark asked and continued to pace. "She probably wouldn't agree anyway."

Mark had never felt more useless in his whole life. What good would it do to dream about marrying Bailey when he'd already failed to keep her safe? That was job number one of a family man. He should have never brought that dog home.

He stopped pacing and the blocks all fell into place. Mrs. Hargrove was right. He had finally reached a problem so big he couldn't fix it by himself. He needed help. Mark looked around. Gabe couldn't help him; he'd already found that out. He didn't know how to be a family man and no one could go back and erase the problems of his childhood. No one could help him.

Then Mark remembered that he'd slipped that pamphlet into the inside pocket of his suit jacket—the simple brochure about God. He'd read it, but he figured he'd give it back to Mrs. Hargrove this Sunday or maybe just slip it back into the stack she had in her classroom without her knowing. It didn't seem right to throw the thing away. No, he couldn't do that.

Mark had his fingers on the pamphlet when the door to the waiting room swung open right in front of him.

"Mrs. Hargrove. Rosie," Mark said in greeting. He left the pamphlet right where it was in his pocket. Before anyone else could speak, Rosie screwed up her face and took off running toward him, her feet tapping along the tile floor and her petticoats swinging. She launched herself at him, forcing him to fall with her tucked against him right into the nearest chair.

"Umph," Mark said as he finished absorbing the hit. By the time they had landed safely, Rosie was in his lap, crying so hard she had the hiccups.

"Easy now," Mark murmured as he rubbed the girl's back. She was curled up against his chest. He felt her gasping sobs and worried she might faint.

Mrs. Hargrove must have decided to get

some coffee, because she had left the room by the time he glanced up.

"It'll be okay," Mark murmured, trying to assure Rosie and him both. He wished he had the hope he was pretending to have for her sake. It suddenly occurred to him that he would have some of that assurance if he had completed the steps in that pamphlet. It was hard to trust God though. He couldn't just run crying to God like Rosie had come to him. Although, right now, he wished he could. God was the only one who could fix the feelings he had inside from his childhood.

Not knowing what else to do, he held Rosie with one arm and kept rubbing her back with the other. Finally her sobs quieted.

He thought the storm had passed. Then she looked up at him and he knew he was wrong.

"It was my fault," Rosie whispered in despair and then the words gushed out of her. "I wasn't supposed to scream for the poor doggie and then I did and Mommy fell. I shouldn't have done it. I was to blame. I wanted to show Billy Baker what I could do with my guard dog and my mommy fell." She gulped. "Is my mommy going to die? Like my daddy did?"

"No, oh no," Mark said as he pulled her closer. He didn't care what the truth was; he only knew what his heart told him. "She'll be better. You'll see."

Rosie caught her breath and collapsed against him again.

"And it was an accident," he said to her. "No one was to blame."

Rosie took a few ragged breaths and looked up at him.

"Not even Billy Baker?" Rosie asked. Mark could tell the storm had quieted because she sounded a little prissy and self-righteous. "We're not supposed to run in the café. He should know that. Maybe it is all his fault. He ran inside before he went outside."

Rosie seemed to be more comforted by that thought than she should be, but Mark couldn't let it stand.

"Your mother wouldn't want you to blame yourself or anyone else," Mark said. "Not even Billy Baker. And you know Billy is fine. The dog is fine."

Rosie didn't answer. She just put her thumb in her mouth. He'd never seen her do that before, but he didn't say anything. She was exhausted.

"Josh said to tell you he's staying on the ranch tonight. Maybe I should drive Rosie home. She'd be fine with Josh," Gabe suggested. "I can come back and get you and Mrs. Hargrove later."

Mark felt Rosie grab on to his shirt like it was a life raft and she was sinking.

"No," she whispered. "I want you."

"She's fine here," Mark said. The truth was he needed her as much as she needed him. "There's a small couch in that corner." He nodded with his head toward the section that was labeled for children. "If she wants to sleep, she can stretch out in there. Anyway, they'll probably come out and tell us something soon. Maybe Bailey will even be okay and we can all go back home tonight."

Gabe didn't answer that. He just lifted his eyebrow and sat down in a side chair.

Mark sat there holding Rosie and trying not to pray. His sense of fair play told him it was presumptuous to be asking God for anything. Maybe Mrs. Hargrove would come back soon and he could ask her to pray. That was a surer way to do things.

After some time Gabe left in search of coffee and Mark felt his leg go numb from Rosie's weight. He didn't mind. Then he felt Rosie stir and decided he should take her back to that couch. He started to flex his leg so it wouldn't collapse when he stood. Rosie seemed to settle back into sleep, but he figured he should still move her so he slowly stood up. His leg felt sturdy enough to make it the few yards he'd have to carry the girl. He carefully made their way to the couch.

Rosie stirred when he laid her down.

"Easy now," Mark said as he took off his suit jacket and covered her with it.

She snuggled into the warmth of the coat for a minute and then she drowsily opened her eyes, looked at him and smiled.

"Will you be my daddy some day?" she asked.

"Oh, sweetheart," he said softly. "I don't know how to be a daddy, but you're going to have a good one someday. I'm going to make sure you find him."

Rosie's eyes measured him calmly. "I can help you be a daddy."

"You can?" Mark asked, surprised.

She nodded and held up one finger. "First, you need to check to see if I brushed my teeth. Oh—" She put her hand over her mouth in alarm and then confessed. "I didn't brush them tonight."

"Tonight's okay," he assured her.

"Then you tell me a bedtime story about a princess," she continued and gave him an admonishing look and put up a second finger. "A good story, not from the newspaper."

"I am sorry about doing that," Mark said. He didn't know what else to say.

Rosie made room for him on the couch and he sat down.

"You can forget about me brushing my teeth if that's too much to do," she said graciously.

"A princess needs strong teeth," he told her.

Rosie nodded. "I guess." She was quiet and then added. "A daddy needs to take care of Mommy, too. But, don't worry, I can help. I'm a good helper."

"Yes, you are." Mark kissed her on the top of her head and her eyelids drifted down. She was asleep again before he could have counted to ten. Mark wondered if she would even remember their conversation when she woke up in the morning. He knew he'd never forget it. It made him want to be a better man than he was.

He slipped that pamphlet out of his suit jacket and took it back out into the main part of the waiting room. He was going to give it another study. This time when Mark read the words of Jesus, his eyes welled up so that he could hardly see Mrs. Hargrove when she came back into the room, two cups of coffee in her hands.

She didn't say anything. She just walked over and set the coffee cups down on the small table. Then she opened her arms and he fell into her embrace like he should have done when he was a child. She sat with him while he said the prayers the pamphlet suggested. Mark asked forgiveness for his sins and welcomed Jesus into his heart.

"I don't know what took me so long," he said to Mrs. Hargrove when he finished. He felt like a new man.

"You came to Him now," she answered. "That's the important thing."

Mark felt his heart ease. "Help Bailey, Lord." It was a relief to be able to ask.

In a while, Gabe wandered back into the room with his own cup of coffee.

Almost on his heels, a white-coated doctor came inside.

"We're moving Bailey Rosen over to the maternity level," the doctor announced. "She's hoping there's a Mrs. Hargrove here. Her breathing coach."

"That's me," Mrs. Hargrove stood up. "Is the baby coming?"

The doctor grinned. "It'll be a few hours." She looked at Mark and Gabe. "One of you the father?"

Mark was tempted, but he couldn't lie. "I hope to be someday, but I'm her good friend."

"I'm her cousin," Gabe said.

"Second cousin, once removed," Mark corrected the man. "To Junior. Almost a stranger to Bailey."

Gabe grinned. "But available."

"I'll stick with Mrs. Hargrove," the doctor said as she started to leave the room. "But if she wants to see either one of you, I'll let you know."

With that, the women were gone and Gabe and Mark sat there.

"My house isn't that far from here," Gabe finally said. "I think I'll go get some sleep. You're welcome to take the bed in my guest room if you want. I have a room for Rosie, too."

"Thanks," Mark said. "But Rosie's sleeping okay on the couch and I won't be dozing off. I'm too wired."

Gabe nodded. "I'll be back in the morning."

Gabe left and a passing nurse dropped off a couple of blankets. Mark wrapped one around Rosie and took the other one to wrap around his shoulders in one of the chairs in the waiting room. He was meant to be right here with Rosie and Bailey, he told himself. They were the closest thing he had to a family and he wanted to be there for them.

On the other floor in the clinic, Bailey felt the cramps coming. The lights were soft and she heard the sounds of machines and then the footsteps of someone coming.

"Did you find her?" she asked the nurse who was looking down at her.

"She's coming."

Bailey felt another pain and gasped.

Then she saw Mrs. Hargrove's familiar face and the older woman took her hand.

"Where's Rosie?" she asked her friend. "And Mark?"

Mrs. Hargrove smiled. "Downstairs in the waiting room. Praying for you."

Bailey leaned up in surprise. "Mark's praying?"

"Especially Mark," Mrs. Hargrove said. "He'll tell you all about it later. In the meantime, we have a baby to welcome to this world."

Bailey nodded. She was ready now.

"Father, thank you," she prayed.

"Breathe," Mrs. Hargrove said and Bailey fell into the rhythm they'd practiced.

It wouldn't be long and she would have a brand-new baby.

Chapter Sixteen

Mark decided every bone in his body ached as he shifted himself once again in the chair. The sun was beginning to rise and he could see a golden rim along the skyline of Miles City. He'd already had five cups of coffee, but his mouth still felt like cotton. He'd checked on Rosie several times and she was sleeping soundly.

He looked out the paned window of the clinic waiting room and smiled.

"Good morning, Father," he prayed. "I'm trusting you with Bailey today. *And Rosie.* And the baby. And me. Help us to be a family if that's what you think is best."

Suddenly, being a family man didn't seem impossible. What was that verse Mrs. Hargrove had told him last night? The one about doing all things through Christ who would strengthen him. That sounded pretty good to Mark. Sort of like having help to go through basic training.

"Help Bailey to see we can do this," he added to his prayer. He knew she might not be willing to take a chance on him, but he had plenty of time. He had already made an offer on Mr. Durham's place right next to the Rosen Ranch. The old rancher was giving it some thought, but Mark was confident.

He heard someone coming into the waiting room and looked up to see a very tired Mrs. Hargrove walking toward him.

"How's Bailey?" he asked, his heart racing. "Please, Father."

The older woman smiled. "The baby's here and Bailey is fine. She wants to see you."

Mark stood up and started to race to the door before he realized. "Wait. What floor is she on?"

Mrs. Hargrove smiled as she sat down and held up his cane. "You might want this, too."

He stepped back and grabbed the cane. He was doing better, but he would need it for any distance.

"The third floor," Mrs. Hargrove answered. "When you get off the elevator there will be a nurse's station. Ask there and they'll take you back."

"Thanks," he called back as he hurried out the door.

He was going to see Bailey; his head rang with the knowledge as he traveled as fast as he could. It wasn't until he reached the elevator that it occurred to him that Bailey might not be ready for the new him or what he had to say about the two of them.

"Lord," he prayed. "Help me go slow."

Then the elevator doors opened on the third floor and he saw the nurse at the station look up with a smile on her face.

"You're Mark?" she asked.

"Yes."

"Second door on the left," she said as she pointed down the hallway. "Keep it to a few minutes. She'll be sleepy."

Before Mark could even nod, he was standing in front of Bailey's doorway. The curtains were drawn, but some light was coming through. Bailey lay on a bed, looking up at him with a sweet smile on her face.

"The baby came," she whispered as she held out a hand.

He stepped forward, took her hand and bent to kiss her on the forehead. "I heard."

"It's a beautiful little girl," Bailey offered.

"I can't wait to see her," Mark smiled back as he squeezed Bailey's hand gently. He had so many things he wanted to tell her, but he could see she was groggy.

"I left word for them to let you see her in the nursery," Bailey said, her eyes starting to close. "She looks just like Rosie did when she was born."

"Double the fun," Mark said softly. "For all of us."

Her eyes closed even though her smile stayed in place.

"I'll come back later," Mark whispered.

"Good," she said so quietly he had to strain to hear the word.

Mark just sat there for a while, holding Bailey's hand and feeling grateful. He had a new daughter for his heart. He was going to have to beg Bailey to marry him now. He didn't know what he would do if she said no to his eventual proposal. But even he knew he needed to give Bailey a little time to adjust to her new baby before he asked her to marry him. He should probably give her a month, he decided. Thirty days was all. He could do that.

Seven days later, Bailey was lying in her bed waking from a nap when she received an engraved invitation to a formal dinner that evening in the kitchen. She smiled as she studied the vellum card that had been tied around the bouquet of red long-stem roses, delivered to her room by a grinning Rosie.

"From Markie," her daughter exclaimed before Bailey had a chance to check for a giver's signature.

"How lovely," Bailey said. She couldn't help but notice that her child's hair was combed and she had a new shiny black bow in her hair. Between Mark and Mrs. Hargrove, her daughter was receiving plenty of attention these days. And Josh had finally been able to leave for Missoula to check on Emma. He hadn't come back yet, but she assumed all was well there, too.

The card went on to say that childcare services were being provided during the dinner hour and the requested attire was a warm robe and nightgown. Mark had probably been reading the book the doctor had given him before he brought her home from the clinic. Pregnant women, it no doubt said, sometimes suffered from depression. The dear man was intending to cheer her up even though she truly didn't need it.

Bailey sighed. That wasn't totally true. She really should be depressed if she had any sense about her. She might need to leave the ranch before long if Emma's child was a boy. She'd still have a half of the ranch and that should translate into some funds, but it might not be much. Mrs. Hargrove had already said she and the children could stay with her until Bailey had a plan, but she couldn't impose for long.

She didn't want to face any of that. Not now. So she floated around the house happily caring for her baby and enjoying Mark's comments as he learned to love their Lord. She strictly refused to look into the future and wonder what she would do without Mark, even though she was more worried about losing him than losing the ranch. He'd said he wasn't going back to the military, but that's all she knew. He cared about her and her daughters; she knew that. But he always said he wasn't a family man and not many men wanted a ready-made family anyway.

She closed her eyes. She supposed she'd have to start worrying about what to do—but not tonight. Tonight she was going to dine in her kitchen with the handsome man who held her heart. She wondered vaguely if there would be music.

She tended to her baby and, a few hours later, she woke from another quick nap to the soft sounds of violin music and the smell of something good cooking. She knew she didn't need to worry about doing more than gathering her best velvet robe around her, but she did have to comb her hair and maybe put on some makeup.

Mark was waiting in his black suit when she stepped into the kitchen.

"Oh," she said as she looked around. Everything was transformed.

The table sat in the center of the room like normal, but it was draped with a white linen cloth. All of the lights were turned off and only darkness shone outside the frosted windows. Instead candlelight made a cozy circle around the table. Tall ivory tapers stood upright in a magnificent silver candelabrum that she didn't recognize. Fine gold-rimmed ivory dinner plates and silverware were set on the table. Linen napkins and crystal goblets completed the table.

"Where'd you find it all?" she asked in astonishment.

"Mrs. Hargrove lent us the things for the table," Mark said.

Then Bailey looked up. White paper pictures of crayon-colored flowers were taped to the cabinets and the appliances all around.

"It's a garden," she said in delight. Reds and pinks and yellows were all over with lush green leaves filling in all the space.

"Rosie's contribution," Mark said with a smile. "She'll need a new box of crayons."

"That's what she's been doing." Bailey knew Rosie was keeping quiet so the baby could sleep, but she had no idea the girl was working so hard.

The timer on the oven sounded and Mark turned back to it.

"The beef Wellington needs to sit," Mark informed her as he slid the roasted beef puff out of the oven. "Special from the café along with some grilled asparagus and twice-baked potatoes."

"I can't believe all this," Bailey said as she twirled. "What's the special occasion?"

Mark seemed to stop briefly. His back was to her though so she didn't know what it meant.

"Oh, I forgot," he said and opened a cabinet to pull out the big red Valentine box he'd been looking at when they were at the café. It must not have been something Josh was buying after all.

Mark held the heart-shaped box out to her and now that she saw the front of it she saw it had a bright green ribbon wrapped around it with a big matching green bow on top.

"Happy belated Valentine's Day," he said.

"Is this to make my heart go?" she asked softly remembering the first Valentine he'd ever given her and how green that one had been. "That's so sweet."

Her heart melted and then she looked up and saw his face. Everything inside her turned to ice. This was not a nice casual dinner. "What's going on?"

"Let's eat first," Mark finally said. "Then we can talk."

Bailey couldn't speak. That sounded like a serious conversation and she was filled with dismay. Mark wouldn't do something like this unless he was planning to leave. He'd want to show her how much he cared and then he'd tell her he was going to say goodbye. They'd be friends forever, he'd say, but he'd be gone anyway. She only hoped he wasn't going to leave tonight.

"The roads still aren't that good," she finally managed to say.

"The pickup gets around okay," Mark answered as he rolled a cart over and put several covered dishes on the table.

"Madam," Mark said as he pulled out a chair for her. She found it strangely comforting that the same patched vinyl showed on the old dining chair he offered. Not everything had been improved.

Bailey sat down. Mark had gone to a lot of work and she had to get through this dinner somehow. He changed the CD in the player before he sat down to the table with her. Everything was ready to eat.

"It smells good," Bailey managed to say.

The food was delicious and she felt like crying. She'd been living in a bubble since she'd come back from the clinic. It felt like all her dreams as a child had come true—it felt like she had a true family. The only problem was that it wasn't so.

"You went to a lot of effort," Bailey said, determined to not spoil all of Mark's hard work. It wasn't his fault she'd let her dreams get away from her. She almost hoped that the baby would start to cry and give her an excuse to leave the table.

"I wanted to tell you," Mark started and then stopped. "I should clear the dishes first. Give me a minute."

She didn't think it took him more than thirty seconds and he was back sitting at the table.

"I wanted to tell you," he started again.

Bailey wanted to close her eyes. "I understand."

"You do?" Mark said, obviously surprised.

Bailey nodded. "You have a life of your own to live and the world is your oyster and…"

"I don't understand," Mark said, frowning now. "I do have a life, but I'm trying to say I want to share it with you and your girls."

"What?" Bailey was shocked.

Mark didn't answer. He seemed to have a script planned and he kept going, "Yes, I want to share my life with you and your girls. I don't want to rush you and I know this seems soon even though we've known each other for years and years. You don't have to say yes or no tonight, but I want you to consider marrying me. I'm in the process of buying Mr. Durham's place. We just have a few details to work out. I'd like you and the girls to move in there even if you don't know if you want to marry me or not yet. You don't know yet, do you?"

Mark looked like he needed to take a breath. Bailey knew she needed one, too.

"Yes," she said when she could speak.

"Yes, you know if you want to marry me?" Mark asked tentatively.

"No," she said and saw him flinch. "I mean yes I know and yes it's yes."

Mark looked stunned. "Yes?"

"Yes, yes, yes," Bailey said until she saw him start to smile.

And then from the doorway, she saw a movement.

"She said yes," Rosie screamed to the whole house.

That seemed to galvanize Mark and he stood up and walked around to where she sat. He held out his hand and she stood up. Then he leaned over and kissed her. Bailey put everything in her heart into that kiss and she got back waves of love in return. She and Mark were family, tied together by bonds of a lifetime.

Then she heard the rapid tapping of little feet and she felt her daughter's arm grab her around one leg. She looked down and saw Rosie had her other arm wrapped around Mark's leg.

The beaming face of Rosie looked up. "Is Markie my daddy now?"

"Soon," Bailey said as Mark bent down and carefully lifted the girl up into his arms.

Rosie sighed as she laid her head against Mark's chest. Bailey had never seen her daughter so content.

"Thank you," Bailey whispered to Mark. Then she stretched up as tall as she could, and he leaned down some, until finally their lips met again. This kiss held the passion of the moment and the promise of a sweet future together. They were a family now.

* * * * *

If you liked this story,
pick up these other heartwarming books
from Janet Tronstad:

Easter in Dry Creek
Dry Creek Daddy

Available now from Love Inspired!
Find more great reads at
www.LoveInspired.com

Dear Reader,

I am pleased you picked up *His Dry Creek Inheritance* to read. I have long wanted to write a Valentine story and am delighted I was able to do so. Bailey and Mark, my heroine and hero, are my favorite kind of couple since they started out as childhood friends.

When you finish this book, you will rightfully suspect that a sequel is coming soon. I have already started the story of Josh and Emma and I can't wait for their happy ending. It will be a few months, so keep looking!

I love to hear from my readers and encourage you to send me a message at www.janettronstad.com or stop by my facebook page (also Janet Tronstad).

Lastly, I hope you have a special Valentine's Day. I always celebrate all kinds of love—friendship, romance, and the love we share in our Lord.

Sincerely yours,
Janet Tronstad